The Mugs & Saucers Café

W K WAITE-GRACIE

ISBN: 978-1-960136-71-8

This book was inspired by an old friend who helped me find my love of words again. Thank you, Amy. A huge thank you to Kim (Sis) and my Abby Girl who encouraged me to keep going and create a series with these characters, knowing how much joy they bring to me. To Gavin, my wee man, who never fails to remind me of my inner beauty and how it spills out and makes all things beautiful when I let my light shine. To my dear grandparents who have both moved on to other realms. I would need to write another book to list all that you have given me, but for this book, I will say I am thankful for your lifelong, unconditional love and support, for passing on the Weird and Wonderful and Dirty, and for being right there, reading over my shoulder. Last, but certainly not least, to the few friends and family members (you know who you are) I shared this adventure with…

*Thank you for cheering me on. My cup runneth over.
Love and Light.*

Come One Sweaty Pie.

Introduction

Maggie Ashberry grew up in the country, spending her days helping her parents run the farm alongside her three younger brothers. She lived a quiet life with the expectation of marrying her long-time boyfriend, Pete, and settling down.

After five years of marriage, and Pete's consistent infidelity, he eventually left her for another woman. Maggie was single and heartbroken, left to take care of her ailing parents and run the family farm, dreaming of adventures from her youth. Then, after the loss of her parents and receiving her inheritance, she packed up her car and cat, left everything she'd ever known behind, and set out on the road. Maggie ended up in a little town in the middle of nowhere, hoping to make a fresh start and finally live independently. She bought a beautiful old house, opened her own bookshop, made new friends, and settled into life happily.

However, just when she came to accept that she would spend the second half of her life single, a familiar name popped up in town that reminded Maggie of snowy cottages and the only time she had truly been in love. Will their paths cross again? Is this stranger her long-lost love, and if so, will three decades apart allow them to reignite the passion they once shared?

Join Maggie as she embarks on a journey of love, friendship, and self-confidence while learning that it is never too late to take risks and find true happiness.

Table of Contents

CHAPTER 1

As Maggie Ashberry locked up the shop for the night, she caught a glimpse of a young couple silhouetted against the glow of the distant streetlight. She smiled to herself reminiscently as they held each other in a tight embrace, recalling those sweet moments that she now savoured from so long ago. The years had gotten away from her quickly, and although she was still a beautiful woman, she hadn't been with a man for many years and had resigned herself to the fact that her days of passionate love affairs were all but a fading memory. Back in her youth, living in the country on her family's farm with her parents and three brothers, she had been coaxed into marrying a "good farm boy" from a "good-standing, local family". Then, although she traveled a bit before college and met and fell in love with another, she felt she was destined to do what she was told and marry Peter Baker, the man of her family's dreams. After all, who else would she even consider marrying in her little town?

He was a decent enough man. Well, as decent as could be expected. He didn't harm her, was kind to her for the most part, had a job, and didn't drink too much or anything like that. Unfortunately, it wasn't long after they were married that he had started to keep to himself. She had her suspicions that he might be playing around, as he had been known to do in their youth, but managed to brush those thoughts aside in an attempt to protect her heart from such a hurtful scenario. Unfortunately, Maggie's attempt at keeping a happy marriage soon crumbled. He eventually stopped taking her places, wasn't spending much time talking to her anymore, and had even stopped showing his affection physically. He eventually spent less and less time at home. Maggie had grown to believe she was no longer attractive enough and that there was something wrong with her. He wouldn't talk to her about it, and she ended up spending most of her energy trying to please him and find ways to make him want her as she thought he once had. After five years of rejection and crying herself to sleep each night, he ended up leaving her for another woman, and she fell into a state of numbness. Maggie robotically filled her days with manual work, helping her parents with the farm. She enjoyed being with the animals and had no problem running the farm with her parents. She had even found a sort of comfort in the quiet of the country, but part of her was missing, empty, like pieces of her had fallen into shadow. She soon let herself forget the parts of herself she had lost.

Maggie broke from her thoughts and her eyes fell upon the couple again as she started her scenic walk home under the blooming saskatoon-berry trees. It had just started to rain. A light, misty rain that added to the nostalgic energy emanating from within her. Spring was ending and the familiar warmth of summer was being carried on the breeze that night. The rain felt warm on her brow, and walking along in the gentle drops of rain had brought her mind back to her younger days. An impish grin crossed her face. She felt a tingling from her head to her toes. Oh, there had been wilder days for Maggie. Freer and happier, lustful days she could suddenly pull from deep within. Like an old, familiar song, one she hadn't listened to for a long time. It was slowly playing in the foreground of her thoughts. To feel the breath of a man whisper her name again, to feel his strong arms wrapped around her… She bit her bottom lip and shook herself out of her brain fog, realizing she had somehow already reached her street.

As she turned down White Tree Lane, the streetlights glinted on the falling blossom petals, landing like a light satin dusting of snow on the pavement. She laughed to herself warmly. *The snow,* she thought while smiling, recalling that old flame and a winter camping trip with friends that had left her head over heels, heartbroken, and wanting to run away from her life forever. *I wonder how life has treated Billy?* she thought. *Wow! It's been so long since those memories were made. Must be, hmmm, 25 years since we last spoke.* Visions and snippets of their intimate moments flashed before her. Their young, unencumbered love felt like a movie she had seen long ago. They met at a ski cabin getaway that Maggie and a few of her friends went on before going their separate ways to university. He was there with a group of friends too, and she found herself drawn to him the moment she saw him. Then, one night in the common area of the cabin, she saw him laughing with a group of people, and felt herself falling for him in a way she'd never known possible. He was strumming a guitar in his lap, his eyes twinkling in the light of the fireplace, and she felt her knees weaken. She remembered thinking, *He's gorgeous! Kinda rugged yet gentle at the same time. Such dark smoky eyes, I could easily lose myself in those.* There had been 15 people staying at the cabin for the week. Some couples shared rooms; others had a few friends bunked up together. Maggie and two girlfriends shared one room, with the guys in their group bunking up in another.

Throughout that evening, Maggie kept sneaking glances at Billy and found herself lost in thoughts of the two of them alone together.

She hadn't realized that he had noticed her watching him. He had spent most of his time watching her too. She recalled wondering if the girl hanging around him was a threat or not, as she always seemed to be with him. Deciding not to worry about the other girl, she continued to watch him and lose herself in lustful fantasies. When Billy got the chance to approach her, he took it. He walked up behind her and with a deep, husky sort of whisper asked, "If I followed you, would you keep me?" She jumped a little as she turned to see him smiling down at her audaciously. She hadn't realized how much taller than her he was, or how broad his shoulders were.

With a grin back, she answered, "I think I might have said yes to that if it wasn't such a crap line!" He was a little taken aback and threw his head back with a chuckle. She had loved the way his eyes smiled when he looked at her. Even after all these years, it felt like yesterday and yet a hundred years ago at the same time. She realized she had stopped dead in the middle of the road, one hand on her heart the other on her throat, lost in a longing sort of trance.

She started down the street again, soon reaching her front garden, opened the gate, and walked up the stone path to unlock her door. Her calico, Bill, meowed as she opened the door. She patted his eagerly lifted head affectionately, smiling down at him. "You're the only man for me, Old Bill," she jested. He purred even louder, weaving in and around her ankles. Shortly after feeding her feline friend, Maggie got ready for bed, then rolled out her yoga mat to do a quick bedtime routine. Old Bill sat on the edge of the bed, close to her, and rolled about while she did a handful of stretches, then curled up in his spot once she finished and settled into bed. More thoughts of Billy drifted through her mind. Another memory of their short love affair played in her thoughts. She remembered how they would say goodnight for hours, kissing passionately against the upstairs landing banister at the cabin. Trying to pull apart and walk away from one another, then pulling each other back in for another make out session while saying goodnight again and again. Maggie breathed in deeply, the memory strong enough that she could still smell and feel his warm skin as she thought of those moments. But like trying to hold smoke in your hands, the harder she tried to recall his smell and touch, the more it slipped away. Snuggling into her pillow, her hands on her heart, she smiled softly. She wished their story had lasted a lifetime. She longed for those moments and wished she could jump right back into those memories and feel that love again. The few men she'd been with never came close. Even though she'd experienced enjoyment with others, they paled in comparison to her time with Billy. Maggie was so grateful for those memories and for the power that love still held for her after so long. *Billy, where has life taken you?* was the last thought she had before drifting off to sleep.

* * *

Rain was steadily falling and rhythmically beating down on the porch roof outside her bedroom. The morning was dark and cloudy, and Maggie pulled the covers up a little higher, listening to the storm. She heard thunder rolling in the distance. A thunderstorm always made her smile. *There's something strangely romantic about the rain and the crackling thunder,* she thought. She was meeting Carla for coffee at the Mugs and Saucers Café later and figured she had better get a move on if she was going to get some work done around the house before heading out. She had bought the house about a year ago, shortly after both her parents had passed away. Two of her brothers had returned home so the three of them could continue running the farm together. She didn't mind running it with her brothers but found it harder to get up each day when it wasn't to help her parents. Maggie's parents had left her a good nest egg, and after receiving the money, she decided she had had enough of farm life and packed up her little black hatchback and her calico cat to let the universe take her where it thought she needed to go. She had spent far too many years in her broken fog and knew she needed to start fresh and start living again.

She found herself more than a thousand miles from the farm when she arrived somewhere deep in the woods, in the middle of nowhere, in a tiny little town called Tamarack. It was incredibly secluded and so deeply immersed in nature. She loved how simple, cute, and friendly the town had felt. It didn't have much, but it had the necessities. There was the main street, which was occupied by a half dozen shops including a grocery store, hardware store, second hand shop, drugstore, and flower shop. There was also a 2-pump gas station, a bar called The Tipsy Turkey, a bed and breakfast, and a restaurant that was owned by a funny old couple. There was a post office, a café called the Mugs & Saucers, and eventually, Maggie's bookshop. There was also old Doctor Trent who worked out of his house at the end of the main street. The town consisted of four paved streets and was surrounded by several farms.

The house that she had bought was a definite fixer-upper, but it had so much character she hadn't been able to resist. It was nestled at the end of the furthest paved street and looked picturesque, set against the big willows, pines, birches, and blossom trees. The moment she saw the house, she felt a strong connection and was instantly drawn to it as if she had always known it. Like a favourite old pair of sneakers, misplaced and eventually forgotten but rediscovered as a perfect fit.

Her favourite things about the house were its big front porch with a porch swing and the big bay window, which soon became hers and Old Bill's favourite place to sit, curled up with a good book and long cuddles. The house needed a lot of work. Most jobs she could do on her own, having grown up with so many brothers and having helped build and run her family's farm. She was no stranger to "men's work". She felt quite at home with a hammer, doing grunt work and finding ways to fix just about anything. There were a few things she could use some help and expertise with, but she just hadn't gotten around to finding the right person for the job. Things had been busy with her little bookshop. Getting set up and collecting enough books to be able to call it a bookshop and getting things organized had taken up most of her time. Although she didn't really need the work too badly thanks to her inheritance, and really didn't make a lot from it, she was enjoying having her own business in such a sweet little town. She had found the community, albeit tiny, was happy to have the cozy little bookshop to visit and rummage through. She called it Ashberry Books - the buy one, bring one, take one shop.

She worked on a few things before hopping in the shower and getting ready to head out to meet Carla. She had first met Carla the day she had arrived. Tired from driving, more than ready for a coffee, and not seeing anywhere she could stop for miles, Maggie was happy when she pulled into town. Noticing the café, she parked her car and eagerly went in. Carla was ordering a triple-triple coffee and a cranberry scone, which Maggie soon learned was her regular order. Maggie lined up behind her and waited, listening as Carla chatted away animatedly to the café owner, a short, round, cherry-faced older woman called Lu. As Carla turned around, she smiled and said "Oh, hullo," to Maggie and headed for a quiet table by the window in the corner by herself.

Maggie ordered herself a black coffee and decided to have the decadent-looking piece of chocolate cake that had been calling her name as she waited behind Carla. After she paid for her cup of joe and took her plate with her piece of cake on it, she walked over to Carla's table.

"Hi, I'm Maggie," she said.

The woman looked up at her. "Hey there, name's Carla," she replied with a smile. "You just passing through?" She indicated for Maggie to sit in the chair across from her.

"Oh thanks! Yes, no, well maybe." She laughed awkwardly as she sat down. "I mean, I'm not sure yet. Actually, I was wondering, is there anywhere I could stay around here?" Maggie motioned out the window with her coffee in hand.

"Well yes, just a few doors down there's Pat and Stan's Bed and Breakfast. Lovely old couple, sure they'd be happy to put you up for as long as you need. Though if you're planning on sticking around, I could help you out there too." Carla had lots to say and asked many questions. She seemed to know just about everything too. Maggie soon learned Carla was the local realtor, among other things, and she quickly introduced Maggie to her lovely fixer-upper. And so, just like that, they had hit it off and became fast friends. Carla lived on a small farm just outside town with her husband Stu. Or as she liked to refer to him: "her main squeeze". Stu didn't leave the farm much except to visit The Tipsy Turkey and run some errands around town. He was quite content just mucking around their farm the rest of the time, finishing his days off by getting pissed and passing out. He was harmless enough and seemed to make Carla happy. He didn't fuss much about what she got up to, which gave her lots of time to do her own thing when she wasn't home helping him with their farm. Maggie thought that might have been one of the secrets to their marriage.

Now, as she neared Mugs & Saucers, Billy crossed Maggie's mind again. Another flash of wild abandon from so many years ago. She smiled to herself as she went into the café. Carla wasn't there yet so she ordered a coffee and sat at their favourite table. It had a great view of the comings and goings without them being too noticeable, but Carla had a good spot to listen in on any juicy gossip she might have missed. However, there wasn't much that Carla missed. Carla liked to stay caught up on all the local news and could be counted on to do so. Taking a sip of her coffee, she noticed "Ain't No Sunshine" playing quietly on the radio and she drifted back to her earlier thoughts of herself and Billy. Their naked bodies tangled in a heated frenzy after Billy had played his guitar and sang to her; when their unquenchable desire for one another overcame them. She was deeply daydreaming until someone bumped a chair as they walked past her with their coffee order, breaking Maggie's thoughts of those days long gone. She picked up her coffee, held it with both hands, and took another sip, feeling her body quiver slightly at the thought of their young, naked bodies. After Maggie had been there for about 10 minutes, the bell on the café door gave a little jingle and Maggie looked up to see Carla walking in.

"Sorry I'm late Mags," she said as she walked past, shaking out her umbrella and heading up to the counter to grab her coffee and scone before heading back and joining Maggie at their table. She slid a couple of pieces of mail across the table and Maggie picked them up. Another one of Carla's many jobs was delivering the town's mail. There wasn't really much today. One of those "you may be a winner" notices and a postcard with a picture of the Sphinx on it. It was from her youngest brother who had been traveling for several months now with some friends. He was obviously in Egypt at the moment, and she smiled to herself thinking of all the fun he was probably having. She flipped it over and laughed.

Never one for saying very much, she thought as she read: "Hey Sis, in Egypt having a blast. Swimming with the crocodiles. I'll get some pictures of the pyramids for ya. Love, Frankie." She laid the postcard down and looked up at Carla who was taking a sip of coffee.

"So, Carla, what have you been up to?" Carla, now taking a bite of scone and chewing it quickly, answering eagerly.

"Been helping a newb find a house! Haven't had to do that since you came into town Mags. Actually, he was quite disappointed to learn 7 White Tree Lane was already taken; seemed to take a real shine to it!" Maggie put her coffee down, looking up at her whimsically.

"Well, I might agree to share it if he's cute enough and can swing a hammer," she joked.

"Actually, he *is* cute! Real cute! Good arse too!" Carla laughed and continued talking in typical Carla fashion. "And he's an all-around handyman. I imagine he's quite good with a hammer. Single too and quite ready to lay down some money for a house. Real catch Mags!" Maggie laughed cynically.

"Ha, ya right, Carla, and I'm a young beautiful ballerina starring in the Nutcracker Suite! We usually get some good catches around here!" She picked up her mug again and took a sip of her coffee with a skeptical look on her face.

"No, for real Mags!" Carla answered. "Said he's looking for work, can fix just about anything. Here, look, he gave me his card!" She grinned a little and with a whistled breath out, added, "What an arse! I was tempted to give those sweet cheeks a pinch myself if I didn't already have my main squeeze wait'n for me at home." She stood up with a smirk, pulled a business card out of her back pocket, and handed it to her. Maggie almost dropped her coffee.

Billy Stanton

GENERAL CONTRACTOR AND HANDYMAN

644 887-4212

Her heart was suddenly in her throat as she asked, "What did he look like Carla?"

Through a mouthful of scone, Carla replied, "Dunno…cute…dark hair…dark eyes…blue, smiley eyes, you know the ones I mean Mags, like he's almost winking cheeky like at ya, sexy smirky sort of smile too, and don't forget, good arse. Great arse!" She took a sip of her coffee, swallowed, and added, "Deep sort of raspy voice too like he could sing the pants right off ya Mags! Mags? Mags? Where'd ya go?" She waved a hand in front of her, and Maggie realized she was gazing blankly, with a sort of dumb-founded grin on her face. *It couldn't be*, she thought to herself, deciding not to mention it to Carla until she was sure whether it was him or not. Carla was always pushing Maggie to land herself a good catch. She had tried a number of times to set her up with the local men, but they weren't really the kind Maggie wanted to settle for. She'd already settled once and felt like there would never be anyone who would come close to her one true love. Carla always insisted that Maggie didn't have to "settle" but should take some of them up on their offers of a good time once in a while. "Gotta clear the cobwebs every so often, you know!" she'd say. Maggie brought herself back from her daydreaming.

"What's that? Oh, sorry Carla, just drifted. Hey, could I keep this?" she asked as she stuck his card in the top pocket of her raincoat. "I've been needing some extra help around the house, maybe I'll give this guy a call and find out what he charges."

Carla was finishing up her scone and taking another gulp of her coffee as she answered. "Sure thing Mags! Be sure to sneak a peek at that arse when you get the chance," she said, winking.

Later, as she was walking home, Maggie couldn't quite believe the odds. *It's just a weird coincidence,* she thought to herself. *I'm sure there are lots of Billy Stantons in the world, he'd be pretty high up in the ranks by now too. Not likely to be a handyman looking for work in a nowhere town. No, couldn't be my Billy! My Billy,* she smiled warmly. *Once upon a time.*

CHAPTER 2

Maggie decided to go into the shop early on Sunday morning. Someone had dropped off a box of books she hadn't gone through yet, and she was curious to see what was in there. There were a dozen or so fishing books, some old Farmer's Almanacs, eight or so cookbooks and baking books, and what looked to be a few well-loved romance novels. She picked one of them up and flipped it over to read the description on the back and chuckled to herself. *Ha, so cheesy, as if things like this actually ever happen in the real world. Well, not for any length of time*, she thought. *Even if you're lucky enough to find passion, they cheat on you or leave you, or the passion puffs out in a cloud of smoke shortly after tying the knot. Or, like for young Maggie and Billy, it lasts one blissful week, and you spend the next 25 years wondering what might have been, settling for another, getting dumped, and then closing yourself off from ever believing true love could exist.* She dropped the book on top of the others, then picked up the box and went over to the computer to add the books to the computer inventory list, printing off their stickers and then giving them their rightful homes on the shelves. After she put the books away, she spent the rest of the morning dusting and tidying up, only seeing a couple of customers who stopped in to chat for a bit before heading back out. In the end, she decided to close up and go home for an early supper.

As Maggie drew closer to her house, she noticed her front gate had come right off its hinges. *Boy, I really do need to spend some more time fixing this place up. Maybe I should shut the shop for a couple of weeks and focus my efforts here instead*, she thought to herself. She walked into the usual happy greeting from Old Bill and enjoyed a little chat and snuggle with him before turning the radio on and making herself a salad and some pasta. Maggie headed out to the back pergola and sat on the little patio to enjoy her meal. The pergola was looking a little weathered as well and in need of some new beams and some fresh stain. She'd have to get up there and replace them before they started to rot. The long strands of ivy were growing higgledy-piggledy, no longer climbing the beams to the top lattice.

As she ate, enjoying the quiet of her yard, she remembered one of the nights at the cabin with Billy and felt her cheeks flush. It was a couple of nights after they had met. Everyone was enjoying good food and music and dancing in the common room. A few of them had decided to make a special dinner with roast chicken and roast beef. Someone had even made Yorkshire pudding, and they had all put extra money in for a few bottles of champagne. They asked everyone to dress up in their fanciest clothes, and the girls had fun getting themselves all dolled up. Maggie had worn a long, black velvet dress with spaghetti straps, along with an electric blue shawl that draped over her shoulders. The shawl made her emerald-green eyes pop. Her golden-brown hair was pulled up in a clip with a few rebellious caramel curls escaping the clip's grasp. She and Billy had been attached at the hips in their few short days together and had already been out snow-shoeing, hiking, and skiing. They had also enjoyed sitting together for hours while he strummed his guitar and sang. They had played endless rounds of charades and Twister with some of the other cabin visitors and had ended their days snuggling by the fire together. That night, in the glow of the firelight with music playing and young happy energy all around them, they were connecting deeper and deeper and falling further in love with each other without even realizing just how far.

As a few of them were dancing to a song that he loved singing to her, screaming and commotion suddenly broke out. They turned in time to see a section of the cabin roof falling down, dropping tiles and snow on top of the few people under it. Hectic laughter and people frantically moving out of the way quickly ensued, and soon there was a snowball fight among the ones left in a small pile of snow. No one was hurt, thankfully, and it was much too late to call anyone to fix the gaping hole that night. Maggie grabbed Billy's hand and said, "Come help me." Billy laughed, thinking she was kidding, but followed her anyway. They couldn't find anything in the cabin, so Maggie pulled on somebody's big boots that were sitting at the door and grabbed a jacket. Billy followed suit, and out they went to the shed that was next to the cabin. Among the shovels, skis, sleds, and snowshoes they managed to find a couple of hammers and some nails and an oddly shaped piece of plywood. They pulled out a ladder and the two of them climbed up onto the snowy roof and managed to mend the hole well enough to keep any more snow from getting in, at least for the night, they hoped.

"You are something else, you know that?" he laughed. "I've never seen such a beautiful woman, in a fancy dress and wearing somebody's old clunky boots nonetheless, be so good with a hammer before," he added with a smirk.

"Ya, well, I'm pretty good at a lot of things," she replied with a grin. They climbed back down into the snow and returned to the shed to put the hammers and ladder away. As Maggie turned around to open the door and lead the way out, he grabbed her hand and spun her around, pulling her up against him. Their eyes met and a fire ignited inside both of them.

"What else are you good at Mag?" he asked her, whispering the question with serious intensity, pulling her in with those dark, smoky eyes. Before she managed a response, they were locked in a tight embrace, kissing each other hard, hands caressing and grabbing at one another, pulling off their jackets. He lifted her up, carried her over to the workbench, and sat her down. Billy stood up against the bench with Maggie's legs wrapped around him, his arms wrapped tightly around her. She pulled herself against him, and as he stood in front of her, he gently slid her straps down her arms, one at a time, kissing her neck and shoulders as each strap fell.

"God you smell good," Billy whispered. Maggie inhaled deeply, shivering, both with anticipation and from his words dancing over her skin. The wintry breeze found its way into the little shed, causing her to shiver again and she pulled him in tighter, undoing his pants. He lifted her from the bench; Maggie stood before him as he kissed his way down the front of her body, grasping her breasts on the way. He slowly undid the long zipper in the back of her dress as he descended, letting the black velvet fall to the floor. His hands found their way to her silky panties and down they came. He slowly kissed his way back up her body, taking his time at the top of her thighs. He kissed her hips and under her navel, then licked his way up before lingering on her breasts, squeezing them as he kissed and licked all the way up to her neck. He then lifted her back onto the bench, letting *his* pants drop to the floor now too. He was so hard and ready to thrust himself inside her. She was so wet and willing to let him enter and with so much more passion and appetite than either had ever experienced. They were suddenly one, writhing and pulling into each other deeply.

"Billy!" She moaned his name over and over as he penetrated and moved in and out of her with gliding intensity, intoxicated by each other's scent and energy. She clawed at his back, letting her hands drop, grabbing his ass, pulling him harder and deeper inside of her, until she felt him let go and she felt the release from within herself. Their bodies quivered.

"Maggie!" He called out her name in her ear as they held each other tightly, hardly moving now, just being, breathing heavily and then leaning into one another, almost laughing with elation. They stayed in the shed for hours, attacking each other again throughout the night. Later, they simply held each other, talking about how they wished they could stay this way forever. Wishing they didn't have to go their separate ways and live their separate lives. She hadn't told him: he was the first she'd ever gone all the way with. He had guessed it but didn't ask her about it. He was surprised, given the raw intensity between them and the speed of her making love with him. Instead, they chose to absorb each other's bodies, as much as they could, in their brief time together.

Maggie recalled fondly how they had found many interesting places and secret opportunities to pounce on each other in the fleeting days that followed. A closet, the shower, a balcony, and an empty bedroom that they climbed into through the balcony window. They seemed unable to contain their insatiable desire for one another. Each time was just as passionate and intense as the last. It didn't seem fair that in just over a week he was headed off to military school and would be in some far-off country in only a month. She too would soon be starting nursing college back home where her betrothed was waiting for her. They had decided not to try to stay in contact, that it would be too difficult, too hard, not being able to be with each other. Billy knew he really wouldn't have the ability to keep a long-distance relationship going as he would be in the thick of military school. There would be no time for a social life for a number of years, and how could Maggie keep a relationship with Billy when she was supposed to be marrying Pete? As they lay there with each other, Billy reached up and undid a gold chain he was wearing from his neck. He put it around Maggie's and did it up.

"I know we've decided to let this week go, but here's a little something to remember me by." She reached up and undid the silver heart locket she was wearing and did it up around his neck. She had only recently gotten it. She hadn't even put pictures in it yet. They pulled each other close and tried to hold onto as much of that moment as they could, keeping each other warm with their naked bodies wrapped around one another. Oh, those memories were still so vivid and tangible. Maggie could almost feel their bodies tangled together still. Now her thoughts turned to the farm. All the years she spent there, so often wishing she was somewhere else. Daydreaming about "would haves" and "could haves". Thinking of what life would have been like if she'd married Billy. All the time she had spent learning to push those thoughts away so that they could no longer touch her. It just made her sad anyway, so why even think about them?

The sun was starting to set when she gathered up her dishes and went back inside. As she was cleaning up she heard a knock at the door. She heard the door open and then came Carla's voice. "Hey Mags, you in there?"

"Yes, in the kitchen, Carla," she answered. Carla came around the corner looking quite exhausted and proceeded towards the cupboard and grabbed a glass.

As she walked to the fridge, she asked, "Mind if I grab a glass of bubbly water, Mags?" Maggie smiled as Carla helped herself.

"Not at all, help yourself." The two friends sat across from each other at the kitchen island, Carla wiping sweat from her brow.

"Just been out helping Stu do some plowing in the backfield for the last five eff'n hours!" She stopped to take a big gulp then continued. "He started getting nasty cuz the plough stopped working, so I said, 'I'm outta here Stu,' jumped in the truck, and booted it over here! Geeze, that man, Mags! Either he's not doing nothing at all or he won't stop what he's doing until he hits the floor! Haa! Pretty much sums him up in all departments!" She laughed to herself. "Sure glad I got'em though! Even if he is an arsehole most of the time. Not sure I'd be happy if he wasn't drive'n me a little crazy. Kinda keeps the spark going. Say, what are you up to tonight?" She sat her now half empty glass down, looking up at her.

"Oh, not much Carla." Maggie answered. "I spent a few hours at the bookshop and thought I might do some work around here, but now that I've eaten, I think I'll just laze around, maybe have a bath, and go to bed." Old Bill hopped up onto the island and rubbed up against Carla's arm.

"Oh, hey Bill the Pill, nice to see you too," she said and gave him a little pat on the head then finished her drink. He turned his tail up at her, meowed, and hopped back down. "You know Mags, you could do with another man besides Old Bill around here!" There it was. Today's addition of Maggie needs a man, brought to you by Carla Myers. "Hey, did you call that good arse yet Mags?" she asked, nudging her arm against Maggie's encouragingly.

"No, not yet… haven't really had a chance," she answered quickly as she got up to finish the dishes.

"Oh, come on, Mags. You gotta get some action. It's not often, well, actually it's never, that a cute, available stranger comes to town." Maggie smiled to herself wondering if he really was a "stranger".

"Ya, you're right Carla. I know, I'll get around to it soon, but just for help around the house." She turned and smiled the most believable smile she could give.

"Alright Mags, but you'll be sorry if someone else makes him their main squeeze instead of you! And ya know, some help around the house could be good for clearing out the cobwebs!" She winked and nudged Maggie with her elbow again. "Well girl, best get back to Stu. He'll be wanting his dinner, if he hasn't already passed out from drinking it." She laughed again, this time at her own joke, and got up and headed for the door. "See you tomorrow, right Mags?" she called as she opened the door. "You still coming with me up to White Lake in the morning, aren't ya?" she asked.

"Of course, I'll see you bright and early." Maggie answered as she closed the door behind her friend and turned the lock. "Time for that bath and some yoga, I think," she said aloud as she headed upstairs for the night.

CHAPTER 3

The next day, shortly before sunrise, Carla arrived in her old red pickup, grinning from ear to ear. She beeped the horn as Maggie came out the front door with her fishing rod and a packed picnic lunch for the two of them.

"All set Mags?" she asked as Maggie opened the squeaky passenger door and climbed in.

"Sure thing Carla; brought us a couple of thermoses of coffee to help perk us up - one black, one with extra cream and sugar already added. I think I'll get started on a cup, how about you?" Carla nodded and Maggie proceeded to pour them each a lid full, and off they went. One of Carla's many "jobs" was selling fish at the grocery store in town. She usually went out three times a week and caught a fresh batch. Maggie always tried to join her on her Monday run. She hadn't really fished before but soon realized there really was something empowering about being in the thick of nature, patiently waiting for a bite and snag'n yourself a big ol'fish! She had grown to look forward to her Monday fishing days with Carla.

Two women out in nature without any cares felt pretty good to Maggie, especially after all the years of not being free. She really did enjoy hanging out with Carla and had found it much easier to fit into such a small town, already set in its ways, because of their friendship. Carla had lived there her whole life, got on with everyone, and knew pretty much everything about everyone at least three generations back. She was full of piss and vinegar and told it like it was, and she had a heart as pure as gold. She didn't put up with any crap either and let you know if she didn't like it. She took Maggie under her wing and always had an opinion of everyone. She tended to ramble on a lot of the time, but Maggie loved hearing her banter. The funny thing was, fishing was really the only time Carla was quiet. She'd fill Maggie in on all the town news on the twenty-minute journey to their favourite fishing hole, sit placidly for a few hours, and then go right back to chattering all the way home. She was quite the woman, and Maggie was certainly glad for her friendship over the past year. She dropped Maggie off for the day with a happy wave out the pickup window, beeping the horn again as she pulled out of the half-circle drive.

"Time for a wash I think. Love fishing day, don't love the smell," she laughed, talking to herself. "Though, Old Bill sure does." She always brought one or two of her catches home to share with the old boy for a treat.

The next day was a beauty. The sun was shining bright, it wasn't too hot, and a gentle breeze was steadily blowing. Maggie managed to rehang the front gate and decided to give it a fresh coat of paint while she was at it. On either side of it ran rows of 4-foot-high hedges that wrapped around her front garden right up to the sides of the house, acting like a fence, so it wasn't a very big job just painting the swinging door. She settled on a light mint green, partly because she liked it, mostly because the only other colour she had on hand was bright red and she didn't really want her front gate to be that prominent. There was another gate around the side of the house that led to the backyard that she decided to paint as well, thinking she might as well make things look like they belonged together. After a quick bite to eat, she started working on the front gardens. They were in desperate need of cutting back and weeding, and it took her the better part of the day before finishing up the job. She was pleased with herself when she stopped and looked around.

Would you look at that Maggie, she thought to herself. *This place is looking not half bad.* She was just thinking about going in for a nice long bath when she heard the familiar rumble of Carla's pick-up pulling into the drive. Maggie went to the gate and opened it before Carla was out of the truck. She didn't want Carla to get wet paint all over her hands.

"Hiya Mags," she called. "What'cha up to?" Maggie held the gate open while Carla walked through. "Wow! Looks frick'n awesome out here Mags," she said, looking around the front garden. "You finally called good arse, eh?" she asked with a smirk.

"No, I didn't. I've been working out here most of the day, on my own. It does look good though, doesn't it?" she added, smiling at her hard work. They walked up the stone pathway and up the steps into the house.

"Oh, come on Mags, just call'em would ya?" Carla coaxed.

"Now don't start that again, Carla! Want some bubbly water?" Maggie asked, washing her dirt and paint-covered hands, then getting glasses out for both of them.

"Sure." Carla answered smiling, sitting herself down at the kitchen island.

"So, what's up?" Maggie asked. "I thought you and Stu were going out tonight?" Carla took the glass and shook her head.

"Nope. He's already pickled. Going nowhere tonight. He went out to use the tractor and couldn't get'er going, kicked and cursed at it for a while, then came in madder than hell, flopped in his chair with a bottle o'whiskey, and pickled himself nice." She took a big gulp of bubbly water and sat the glass back down. "So, thought I'd see what you were up to." The two friends ended up sharing dinner and watching an old black and white movie, one of Carla's favourites this time. It was *The Haunting*, an old classic horror movie that was not one Maggie would have picked, but Carla always put up with her cheesy love stories so she gave in. Maggie was totally spooked by the time it was over and made Carla stay for quite a while before letting her drag herself off of the comfy old chair in the corner that she'd claimed as her favourite and finally heading home. She laughed at Maggie as she was leaving.

"Awe Mags, see, you need a hunk to save you from the boogie man!" she said, chuckling as she went out into the night. Maggie gave her a look and promptly closed the door, quickly locking it behind her. She decided to keep a few lights on, just to be safe. She tidied up a bit, more to keep herself occupied and to stall, before finally heading up to bed and was glad to have Old Bill following her up the stairs when she finally braved it.

CHAPTER 4

Time marched on. Maggie slowly but surely finished a few more things around the house. She had ordered some beams to fix the pergola from a lumber store in the nearest county. It would be quite some time before they were ready, and she would need to arrange to pick those up. So, she decided to work some more on sprucing up her home sweet home. She had repainted the front porch and patched a few loose floorboards. Then she decided to paint her front door the same light minty green to match her front and side gates. She stepped back and admired her home. It looked so pretty, nestled among the bright leafy green trees that encircled the house; though, she had noticed a few of the leaves already starting to change colour. *Time really does move faster with age*, she thought to herself, *Autumn will soon be here. Best keep at it.* She loved autumn - the changing colours and the smells of nature getting ready to sleep for the winter was magical to her. Here in the middle of nowhere, surrounded by nothing but trees, it was just so beautiful. She looked forward to the coming months.

It was around this time that she arrived last year, and the town had looked so perfect amongst the oranges and reds surrounding it. She was eagerly anticipating being in her own place to enjoy it this year. The next project she hoped to tackle was her kitchen. Some of the cabinet doors were already coming off and others weren't far behind. The old wallpaper was peeling, and the sink had a steady 10-minute drip after every use. Despite all that, Maggie really loved her old fixer-upper and was enjoying rebuilding it with her own two hands. Maggie had posted a notice at the shop to let her loyal customers know she was closing for a two-week holiday. She hoped to get quite a bit done by that time - at least enough to make her home look and function a little better before Tamarack was covered in its annual blanket of snow.

Again, Maggie's thoughts drifted back to fond memories with Billy. One morning, Maggie and Billy decided to sneak away together. Dressed in their warm coats, hats, and gloves, Billy grabbed his guitar and the two headed out to the trail looking for a secluded spot to practice singing together. Although it was cool, the sun was strong and bright, and they sat under a tree while Billy played his guitar. The two of them singing favourites together, falling head over heels for each other. The music weaving their already intense energy into a stronger connection. An energy they couldn't begin to understand in their youthful days together. As Billy sang "Ain't No Sunshine," Maggie became more smitten by the moment. They went from happy, lighthearted hanging out to locking eyes and a sudden, intense need to be one. Billy sat his guitar against the tree and Maggie crawled towards him in the snow and sat straddled on his lap. They looked at one another with hungry eyes. Maggie could feel the warmth of the sunshine on her face as she remembered that moment. As their lips pressed together, she felt warmth run through her whole body. She wrapped her arms around Billy tightly as they kissed deeply, they were soon undoing each other's pants and Maggie climbed back onto Billy's lap. She slid down over top of him. They watched one another, holding each other's faces as she lifted herself up and down, riding him with such pleasure. She was soon crying out with delight. Billy's hands sliding down and lifting her quickly, up and down.

"Ohhh." Maggie moaned, bouncing with satisfied enjoyment.

"You're so hot Mag," Billy groaned as he felt her cumming. They could hear friends talking and laughing somewhere on the trail, their hearts racing as Billy reached climax. "Awww." His release, explosive. Kissing passionately as he finished. Their bodies shivering with orgasm and from the coolness of their snowy retreat under the trees. Maggie shivered thinking about it. That familiar angst to relive those delicious moments engulfed her thoughts again. She knew what they had together was special and dreamed of those precious moments again and again. A feeling of loneliness swept through her. *How did I end up single and sad?* She wondered. *If I could turn back time, I would…I don't know, I wouldn't have gotten into that cab and left him? I would have gone home with him? Who's to say it would have worked out? The grass is always greener Maggie.* Maggie put her hands on her heart and closed her eyes. *Maybe I can manifest a man just like him into my life?* She laughed, almost crying. *Who am I kidding? There will never be a man as wonderful as my Billy.*

The days progressed and so did Maggie's work. She was right in the thick of her home's reno and was on such a roll that she had even declined her usual Monday fishing morning with Carla the first week. By Thursday, Carla called begging her to take a break and saying, "You gotta at least come for a coffee with me Mags!" Maggie didn't really want to stop her momentum but was missing her friend too and decided to meet her at the Mugs and Saucers Café.

Carla had lots of gossip to bring her up to date on. The market where she sold her fresh-caught fish was now requesting a double order,

"On account of the local vet making his own pet food now and needing to buy fish from the market." Then there was "Old Pat from the bed and breakfast. She hired young Beatrice, you know, Ben the dairy farmer's oldest daughter, the one with the funny eye, to help run things while old Stan was in the hospital recuperating after his heart surgery." Maggie smiled and sipped at her coffee while Carla filled her in and munched on her usual cranberry scone. Carla chattered away for over an hour. Maggie really didn't mind listening to all her stories; they were always, at the very least, entertaining - plus it kept the spotlight off of her.

"Oh Mags, did you hear the post office had a fire? Quite the ordeal for the old ladies, that's for sure. Cranky old Mrs. Slade brought her husband to work; seems he's get'n a little forgetful, so she's having to keep'em with her if she's gone too long. Well, he tried warming up a muffin or something in the microwave in a tinfoil cup!" She laughed and a few specks of scone escaped. Maggie grinned. "Ya, the whole inside of the oven was ablaze, old ladies flying out the door screaming and hobbling." She took a gulp of coffee and laughed again. "Apparently Mrs. Slade took a broom to the old fella, yelling curse words at'em the whole way home." Maggie laughed too; the image was quite comical. Mrs. Slade always had big pink curlers in her hair, covered with an old, worn out handkerchief, and Old Mr. Slade usually followed along behind her, always in his slippers, shuffling along no faster than a turtle. No one was really sure if he was ever even awake or not. The image of the two of them running along, broom in Mrs. Slade's hand, curlers bouncing, and him trying to move faster than his usual shuffle and still keeping his slippers on with his hands over his head made Maggie giggle out loud.

Maggie had promised Carla she would go fishing with her the following Monday, and just before the break of dawn the next week, she arrived with her usual smile and waved out the old truck window. "All right Mags?" she asked as Maggie dropped her rod and net into the back of the truck and climbed in.

"Sure thing, just a little slower than usual this morning!" she answered with a slightly pained laugh. "Oh, my butt and legs are really feeling it today after climbing up and down the ladder so much the past few days! Phew, really noticing my age this morning, that's for sure." She buckled herself in and rested her head back against the seat.

"You know Mags, just a thought of course, but there's this guy that does handy work that you could call up and ask for help," Carla said grinning, followed by a little wink.

"Oh, good one Carla. I'm fine, just stretching some muscles I haven't used much in recent years!" Maggie replied with a fake smile. Carla laughed.

"Or I could hook you up with a strapping farm boy?" Carla added, but seeing the look on Maggie's face, she dropped the subject, and they each enjoyed their cups of coffee as the old truck rumbled along the dirt road to their fishing spot. Carla had brought her canoe this time, hoping to catch more fish out in the middle of the lake, rather than their more frequented spot on the big rock under the large willow tree. It was a lovely morning. Bright and sunny and not as hot as it had been. The breeze was definitely starting to feel more like autumn, and it made sitting out in the canoe quite comfortable. With the double order for the grocery store, Carla was hoping to catch some extras while she had Maggie out with her. The two of them sat almost completely in silence for a couple of hours and managed to catch a fair number of fish before calling it a day and heading back to the dock.

"Actually, you know what Carla?" Maggie asked as they drove down the main street, back into Tamarack.

"What Mags?" Carla replied, beeping her horn and waving at someone on the street.

"Well, maybe you should set me up with someone." Maggie said. Carla hit the brakes and gawked at Maggie.

"You feeling alright Mags?" Maggie laughed looking at Carla's dumbstruck expression as she asked the question.

"Get out of here, yes, I'm feeling alright. Just, I don't know, a bit lonely I guess." And before Carla could say anything else, she quickly added, "Someone normal, clean, and between 40 and 50 years old Carla." Maggie gave her friend a serious look, then smiled at her.

"You got it Mags. Give me a couple of days to scout around for ya!" She was beaming. "Aw, Mags, wouldn't it be great if you and your new fella and Stu and I could start hanging out together? Be nice to get a little action too, eh Mags!?"

Maggie was already regretting this can of worms she'd opened.

"Say Mags, you feel like a girl's night tonight? You know, before you get back into your house renos again?" Carla asked almost pleadingly. "I could use a break from Stu! Not sure what's gotten into him lately. He's even more tired than his usual self, not even look'n for a roll in the hay! I could sure use a break from look'n at his old mug for a night." How could Maggie say no to that?

"Sure, sounds good to me. What do you want to do? Mugs and Saucers? Moonlit skinny dip? Some nicky nicky nine doors? A chick flick and pizza? Dance party? What'll it be, Carla?" Maggie asked with a smile.

"All sounds perfect Mags, let's decide later. Got some running around to do and then I'll pop back into yours." They had just arrived at Maggie's driveway. Maggie hopped out and grabbed her things.

"Okay, see you later." Carla beeped the horn and off she went.

Maggie decided to make a couple of pizzas after she got cleaned up from fishing. Even if they didn't eat them tonight, she'd have them ready for the week ahead. She had the radio playing as she kneaded the dough, rolled out two big circles, and topped them just the way the two friends liked them. Maggie's with mushrooms, olives, and extra cheese. Carla's with pepperoni, onions, and sausage. "This Magic Moment" came on the radio, and she turned it up and danced while she finished up the pizzas. Her mind wandered once again back to those few short days spent with Billy. The night they first attacked each other was the night a few of them had made dinner for everyone, and she smiled to herself thinking of all of them in the kitchen together. There had been much laughing and talking, some of them chopping up veggies, others making sure that they had all they needed for mixing drinks. Couples kissing and hugging, friends horsing around, and a short food fight with the grapes occurred midway. *Oh, youth. So quickly you are gone.*

She was cleaning up her pizza prep now, popping a dozen cans of bubbly water into the fridge, and decided to get the chocolate cheesecake she'd been saving out of the freezer when she was back to thinking about Billy. *You know, you just might be obsessing a bit, Maggie.* She put the cheesecake down on the counter and found herself walking over to her raincoat and pulling out the card Carla gave her. She was on her way back to the kitchen, hand reaching out for the phone, when she heard a knock.

Then the front door opened and she heard Carla's familiar, "Hey Mags, it's me."

Maggie shook herself from her thoughts, pocketing the card, and called back, "In the kitchen Carla," as Carla came around the corner and plunked down a half-pack of beer on the counter.

"Hope you don't mind Mags, feeling like more than bubbles tonight." She sat down on her usual stool at the island. "Oh good, you made the pizzas anyway!" Maggie grabbed the six-pack and slid it into the fridge.

"Of course! I love a pizza and beer night with you," she answered as she closed the fridge door. "So, should I start the pizzas now, and we can pop in a movie while we eat?"

Maggie turned the oven on to preheat and sat at the island with Carla. "Sounds good, Mags." The two chatted while they waited for the pizzas and then enjoyed two of their favourite movies over laughter, pizza, and beer. "You know Mags, that 'Singing in the Rain' movie isn't half bad. You know, for one of your sappy love stories, that is." Carla grinned and rolled her eyes at Maggie dramatically. Maggie laughed at her friend.

"Admit it, you like the sap." Maggie teased back. It must have been 1 AM when Carla left, so Maggie didn't bother tidying up. She called for Old Bill, who had meowed grumpily a couple of hours earlier before sauntering off somewhere. No reply came, but when she walked into her room, he was already sleeping on his corner of the bed. He looked up, one sleepy eye winking at her, and gave a little meow while laying his head back down.

"Goodnight Old Bill," she said as she turned off her bedside lamp, laid her head down on her pillow, and was soon fast asleep.

She slept later than she had hoped and was feeling a bit lazy the next morning, so she grabbed a big cup of coffee and headed for a cool shower to wake herself up before getting started on some more projects. She hadn't remembered how she'd almost called Billy yet and was already well into clearing out the kitchen cupboards and taking off the doors to repaint them when he popped back into her head. She stopped for a moment, tempted to call, but decided it wasn't likely to be "her Billy" and that she didn't really need help with the cupboards anyways. She plugged along for most of the day, stopping a couple of times for some snuggles with Old Bill. Then she took a couple of leftover pieces of pizza out back and enjoyed a break in the fresh evening air. *That's enough for today,* she thought to herself, as she cracked open a bubbly water and watched the sunset.

CHAPTER 5

By the end of the week, Maggie was pleased to have checked off most of her "to-do" list. The kitchen was done, cupboard doors back up and painted a pretty shade of cobalt blue. There was new white and grey marble tile on the backsplash, and she had even fixed the leaky faucet. She managed to get the bathroom repainted and spruced up and had given the spare bedroom a fresh coat of lemony yellow paint too. All she really wanted to do now was the front hall and staircase. She had ordered a chaise lounge for the front hall and a wardrobe too but they wouldn't arrive for another week, so she wasn't feeling any real urgency to be climbing ladders again quite yet. She would paint out there in a few days and give her butt and legs a bit of a break for the time being. She was back to work at the bookshop the next day and felt quite sure that a lazy evening, soaking up the last of the sunshine, having a bite to eat, and then taking a long bath and getting a good night's sleep was well deserved. She really didn't have a lot left to do and the few things that *were* left would have to wait anyway. There was still the pergola to repair, but she hadn't gotten a call about the new beams coming in yet. And the list of things left on the outside of the house would have to wait until she called someone to help her.

It was nice to get back to the shop. Her regulars were happy to chat with her again and she even managed to sell a half dozen books the first week back. She had changed her schedule from four to two days a week plus one evening so that she could continue working on the house. She had been able to finish up the front hallway and stairway a couple of days before the furniture had arrived. The weather was starting to cool considerably at night now, and the leaves were changing steadily on the trees. She met Carla at Mugs & Saucers late in the afternoon one Thursday after closing up for the day. They hadn't had their usual "coffee catch up" for a while now as Stu was still, well, "Stu-ing" about his old plow, not bothering with much of anything in the way of work and mostly just staying pickled.

Carla was busier than ever, taking over most of his jobs on their little farm along with keeping up with all of her own jobs. She had a few choice words about him and managed to vent a bit before asking Maggie what was new with her. Maggie filled her in on what she'd finished around the house and mentioned that she had finally called "that contractor" but hadn't heard back from him.

"Do you mean good arse? Oh, shit Mags, forgot to tell you, he isn't at Pat and Stan's anymore! Left about a week or so ago now. Apparently, he said he was moving on, on account of not being able to buy a place. Said he was going to head further north and have a look at some forest property, hoping maybe to just build himself a little place." Maggie felt her stomach drop. She had waited too long just like Carla warned her would happen. Now, she'd never know if it had been her Billy.

"Oh, well that's fine. I'll just have to find someone else to help me with the big stuff at the house," was Maggie's response. Carla knew her friend was disappointed and decided not to mention that she'd told her so.

Maggie was back to feeling numb, robotically working between home and the bookshop. She kept herself busy so she could move her focus off Billy whenever he drifted into her thoughts. *You knew your days of love were over*, she'd think to herself. *Why should you be surprised to miss a potential opportunity? Chances of it being "him" were next to none anyway.* At least Old Bill was happy with more cuddles. He loved having more time with her and she settled back into life, as it was before, quite easily.

There was an autumn gathering the following Saturday which, according to Carla, consisted of a farmers' market, beer tent, barbecue, some fair games, and bring-and-buy tables. There was even a little band of locals playing their guitars and banjos and whatever other instruments they could add to the mix put together by the town's little watering hole, The Tipsy Turkey. Carla said it was nice for the town to close up so that everyone could just hang out for the day, and there was always good food and fun. Maggie was reluctant to go but Carla begged and begged. "Oh come on Mags! I haven't had any fun for ages now. Been working my arse off and Stu won't come out with me for any fun either! Say you'll come with me Mags? I can point out a few of the fella's I've got lined up for ya too." So, Maggie gave in.

The market day was good. Lots of families brought fresh vegetables from their farms along with things like baked goods to sell. Homemade goodies, crafts, and lots of bring-and-buy items. It was mostly just an excuse for the town to come together and catch up on any gossip they may have missed and eat and drink. Maggie brought a box of books for the rummage table that she couldn't seem to shift. *They'll probably end up back in the shop*, she thought, chuckling to herself. Carla arrived a bit later than planned but Maggie was happily surprised to see Stu with her!

"Hey, there's Mags!" She heard Carla shout from across the street. The three of them found a nice spot under an old tree to sit and enjoy a coffee. Stu seemed to be back to his old self, laughing and grunting, grabbing Carla's bottom any chance he got, and sneaking a few swigs of whiskey between beers.

Maggie ended up having a good time after all, dancing and eating and visiting some of the town's oldies. She gave in and danced with a couple of men Carla pushed her way, but realized quickly they were not her cup of tea. For life or clearing the cobwebs. Although Carla was eager to set Maggie up, there just didn't seem to be anyone who could fill the shoes Maggie's fond memories had created. She knew her expectations were high, and that they were likely unrealistic as well. Yet, she also felt like she shouldn't lower her expectations. She deserved to be happy, didn't she? So much of her had changed and awakened in that one week of her life. Of course, Billy was the perfect man in her mind. They only had fun together and were the best versions of themselves because that's all they had had time to experience. She had fun dancing with Carla's top picks but graciously turned down their attempts at pursuing her.

Most of the town showed up, many just sitting in their lawn chairs watching a few little ones running about, and the old folks happily enjoying watching them play. Maggie found the music was fun and lively, and it felt good to loosen up and enjoy herself a bit. She did call it a night though when they switched from the live band to the radio and an old Blue Rodeo song came on.

"Gonna head off Carla," she had told her friend, not mentioning that the song that had just come on had snapped her out of her fun and time-warped her back to the love of her life playing his guitar and singing to her. She wished "her Billy" was there with her and decided that she just wanted to get home and cuddle up with Old Bill. It was getting late anyway, and Stu was pickled just enough to fancy some dancing with his little woman. Maggie didn't feel like standing around by herself or having to dance with any of the town's "picks of the litter." Some of that litter had started up with the typical "all the girls are prettier at closing time" glares in her general direction. Carla had been on guard for the last hour or so, ever since "Puts-Out Pauline" had shown up.

"Hell, I'm sure glad to see her back in town!" she complained with sarcastic venom. "She's been watching Stu and flashing her crooked smile at him Mags! I best keep an eye on'em. You know, she's not screwing anybody in particular right now, so she'll be sniffin' around for her next victim! Skanky piece'a'work that one! Prefers the company of another woman's man you know! You're lucky you don't have to worry about that." And off she went to reel Stu in for the night. As Maggie said goodnight and headed in the opposite direction, she heard Carla calling out after her, "See you tomorrow, Mags." Then, as Maggie turned away, Pauline stepped out in front of her, stopping her in her tracks.

Maggie smiled automatically and said, "Oh, sorry," trying to walk past her.

Pauline stepped in front of her again. "You must be the bookshop woman, eh? I haven't been around for a while, but I grew up here, know everyone; don't know you though." Then she gave Maggie a sizing up, sticking her chest up a little higher and her butt out a little further, swinging her bleached-blonde hair off of her shoulders. She was younger than Maggie but the years of having a good time definitely showed. Maggie thought she looked kinda leathered and weathered.

"Yes, that's right," answered Maggie, "I own the bookshop." She tried once again to step around her but Pauline stopped her with a sly smile and continued talking.

"Hear you're not the only new one in town? Fine dish been staying at Pat and Stan's. Noticed him feasting his eyes the other day." She traced her hands along her curves as she said it. "Just might have to introduce myself. Not often you find a man around here with good taste." Then she gave Maggie a look of pity and disgust and sauntered away. Maggie didn't bother telling her "the fine dish" had left town. She really didn't feel like engaging with her at all. *Well, she's a treat!* she thought to herself as she left the lights of the autumn dance and headed home.

Maggie arrived home to a hungry and complaining Old Bill, so she got him fed quickly and gave him a little rub. She was still feeling super full herself since she'd enjoyed a little too many of the baked goods. She made herself a cup of tea and headed upstairs for the night. Of course, starting again down the old track of Billy thoughts. She was just beginning her "what might have been" thoughts but snapped herself out of it. She had left a message saying she was looking for some help with her old house, and left her name and number, so if it was him, he'd be sure to call. *Maybe he wouldn't even remember me. After all, we were kids, a lifetime ago…. One week out of more than 40 plus years of life. There's no way he remembers me.* She sat on the edge of her bed, feeling herself wilting. *That's enough Maggie. Quit before you fall back into your numb fog again.* That was the last thought that she remembered telling herself before climbing into bed with a favourite book and drifting off to sleep.

The next morning, she awoke to Old Bill standing on her stomach, howling his seemingly "close to death" hunger at her. "Ok, ok Bill," she said to him, giving him a pat on the head and then moving him onto the bed beside her. He kept meowing at her until she sat up and looked over at her alarm clock. It was already going on 10:30. *No wonder he's so hungry*, she thought to herself. It wasn't really like Maggie to sleep in so late, but it had been awfully late when she finally fell asleep in the wee early hours. She placed her feet on the floor, grabbed her housecoat, and headed for the door; Bill ran past her and down the stairs expectantly. She followed him, yawning and stretching her arms up. She could hardly pour his food fast enough with his head excitedly pushing against her hand.

"Easy Old Bill, here you go." His face was right in his bowl, gobbling up his long-awaited breakfast. She was glad it was Sunday and she could take it easy. Grabbing herself a coffee and heading back up to the bathroom, she took her time waking up and enjoyed a long bubble bath after a few sun salutations. Then she went back downstairs and grabbed a second cup of coffee. She spent most of the day curled up with Bill on the couch, watching her "go-to" black and whites. *Sabrina*, and a couple of old *Sherlock Holmes*, before finally finishing up with *Breakfast at Tiffany's*. Bill complained when she left the couch, but soon found a spot that was still warm and curled up again happily. Maggie made herself some toast and a cup of tea and enjoyed them out back in the fading light of the day and went to bed early.

CHAPTER 6

Maggie had decided to get out of the house and go into the shop that Monday morning to clean up a bit. When Carla arrived to go fishing, Maggie went out to let her know that she had to go into the shop. Carla was disappointed but said, "No worries, Mags; if you gotta work, you gotta work. I best get rolling." She then gave her usual honk and a wave as she headed down the driveway. Maggie took her time walking, enjoying the fresh morning air. When she arrived at the shop, she closed the door and looked around, wondering where to start. Eventually, she thought that she might dust and vacuum and go through any new drop-offs that might be waiting for her. She left the sign turned to closed as she didn't usually open on Mondays. She really just wanted to get out of the house and try to keep her mind off of Billy.

She still couldn't believe she had missed her opportunity. What if it *had* been him? What if she had missed her chance at being with her true love again? *No*, she thought, *I came in here to get my mind off of this subject! No sense crying over spilled milk, as they say.* She walked over to the radio and flipped it to her favourite station. "Beautiful Sunday" was playing, and she found herself unable to keep from moving to the beat while she started on her chores. She turned up the radio a little and headed for the back shelves to start on the dusting. She worked and danced away for quite some time. She didn't even hear the door open as she was dancing around dusting books and singing away, but suddenly she felt such a strong tingling sensation throughout her body that she paused for a moment, listening. Before she could do anything else a voice spoke.

"You know, if *you* were a library book, I'd definitely check you out!" She dropped the book and the feather duster she was holding, frozen to the spot, and thought to herself, *Deep raspy voice, crap pickup line, it must be… It can't be. I've lost it completely this time.* She took a deep breath and turned on the spot. There he was. An actual, dreamed-up, Billy-like phantom. She'd gone off the deep end; although, her imagination had conjured up a very good apparition that definitely did him justice, even after all these years. Just as gorgeous as he was the first time she met him, smiling cheekily at her. *I really need to see someone about this,* she thought.

And then, as he unbuttoned his jean jacket and smiled affectionately at her, he spoke again, "Hey Mag." Her heart was pounding so hard she was sure he could hear it. *Yes, Maggie, the figment of your imagination can hear your heartbeat!* She shook her head; closed and opened her eyes. He was still there, and he was drawing nearer. She couldn't move. She must be hallucinating. He was inches from her now. She could smell him. *Oh God, he smells so good.* She thought. *This is for real. He's real. It's really him.* She still couldn't move.

"Sorry, I didn't call you back. I thought it must be a mad coincidence when you left your name in the message, and I just had to see for myself." Maggie still hadn't moved yet. She just stood there, looking up into the deepest and kindest blue eyes she'd ever known.

"It's really you," was all she could manage. "But how are *you, here?*"

she asked him. He reached out his hands and gently held both her arms, giving them a little squeeze.

"It's really me, and damn, Mag, it's really *you*." He smiled, shaking his head in disbelief. She didn't know how long they stood there, just looking at each other. 25 years between them and yet it was like no time had passed at all. "You look as beautiful as you did the day you left. Oh, how I've thought of that day. Mag, you wouldn't believe me if I told you how often," he said with a regretful sort of smile. She smiled understandingly back, finally able to move and found his hands now holding hers as she held back tears.

She answered, "Billy, you know, I think I might have a fairly good idea just how many times the thought crossed your mind! Oh, and by the way, your pickup lines are still crap." He laughed that laugh she'd heard in her memories so often. She loved it when he laughed like that - like she took him by surprise and had coaxed it suddenly from deep within when he least expected it.

"Glad to hear that. I was afraid you wouldn't remember me." How could he even think that? She couldn't believe he remembered *her*! They continued to stare into each other's eyes, not speaking, just holding each other up.

"Wow!" she said. "It's so good to see you!" Then, as the universe would have it, "Ain't No Sunshine" came on the radio. A waterfall of warm, electric energy enveloped them. Memories cascaded down upon them as they grinned at each other. Then, without words, without hesitation, he slipped one hand out of hers and curled it around her waist, finding its old, familiar place on the small of her back. She reached up her free hand and wrapped her arm around his shoulder, and they started swaying. It felt like they were the only two people in the universe. They were dancing while the world stood still.

As they were looking into each other's eyes, she felt his hand leave her lower back and gently rub up and down her spine, then comfortably finding its way back down and resting just above her hips. She traced her fingers across his shoulder to the bottom of his neck, up into his hair, and down again. She could hardly stand how beautiful this moment felt. The warmth from his strong body. His breath rose and fell in his broad chest. His large, strong hands so tenderly held her. They were now wrapped in an embrace, her head resting on his chest. Still dancing slowly, he was singing "Ain't No Sunshine" in her ear, and she felt a single tear escape as she smiled and hugged him closer to her. Softly singing along. They danced, holding each other like that for an hour or more.

"Vanilla and lavender." Billy inhaled and said softly. "You always smelled so good Mag." he added, his face moving into her hair gently. Maggie hugged him tighter. She could hardly stand how amazing it felt to feel him pressed against her again. Just holding on, swaying to the music. Whether it was a slow or fast song, they just kept swaying together. "Till I Kissed Her," "Rave On," "California Dreamin'," and "Crimson and Clover." They were lost in their own little world. Lost in their old memories, inhaling the scent of one another that they had only been able to pull from an almost three-decade-old memory. If this was her last day on Earth, she could have gone quite happily. There were no words to express the sheer perfection of their two souls, reconnected with one another. They might have stayed like this well into the night, if they hadn't been interrupted by old Mr. Slade as he slowly shuffled along toward them in his slippers. He was soon followed by Mrs. Slade, curlers bouncing and hollering at him "not to run off on her like that!"

Then, noticing Billy and Maggie standing there together, pulling away from each other, she looked right at Maggie and said, "Oh, well hello Ms. Ashberry; please do excuse me. I don't think you need my husband, as well as whoever this man is too," she said in an uppity sort of tone, waving her hand at Billy and giving Maggie a once over and turning back to look down her nose at Billy. "Didn't realize you'd turned the bookstore into a brothel," she added. She gave Mr. Slade a hard nudge out, and with a goofy smirk on Mr. Slade's face and a last nasty glance back over her shoulder, out they went. Mrs. Slade smartly closed the door to the bookshop behind them. Maggie and Billy stood there silently for a moment, then burst into laughter. They sat down in the comfy reading nook chairs behind them.

"Hope I haven't caused any problems for you Mag," he laughed. "You'll be the talk of the town for sure." Maggie laughed again, but the thought of being the newest news in town didn't matter much to her. She had too many burning questions for Billy to care about Mrs. Slade. She always found something to turn her nose up at anyway.

"How bout we get out of here and catch up, Billy?" she suggested. He nodded at her. She hopped up out of her chair, smiling, and walked over to the radio and turned it off, grabbing her keys and coming back to Billy.

"Sounds like a great idea. Let's get out of here." They left the bookstore, Maggie locking up behind them.

"It's only about a 10-minute walk," she said, smiling at him. So, Billy decided to leave his bike at the shop and come back for it later, grabbing his helmet and his guitar and taking them with them. Maggie smiled at the sight of Billy holding his guitar, seeing his eyes twinkle when he noticed her grinning. "Glad to see you're still strumming," she said to him as they started down the street.

"Ya, maybe we can play something together later?" Her grin

faltered slightly. "You don't play anymore?" he asked, looking a little disappointed.

She shook her head, "No, I still play. I just don't have a piano to play on." Billy's head tilted, looking at her with sadness.

"That's too bad. You played beautifully." She smiled at him, remembering their music-making days.

"Wouldn't fit in the hatchback," she added, laughing and lightening things up again. He grinned back at her as they made their way to the end of the main strip and turned down the next street. "It's a lovely walk," she told him as they walked towards her street.

"Nicer walking it *with* someone though. Funny, all the times I've reminisced and imagined you walking next to me, and now here you are." He smiled coyly at her. They walked, without talking for a few minutes, then Maggie broke the silence.

"I didn't know you rode a motorcycle, Billy," she said. Then she laughed inwardly thinking, *Well of course I didn't know, how could I?* There was a lifetime of not knowing between them.

"I'd love to take you out sometime," he said, grinning at her. As they drew closer to number 7 at the end of White Tree Lane, Billy reached out and took Maggie's hand in his, stopping her. She turned and looked up into his face and smiled back at him. She pulled back and turned, placing his hand behind her and up onto her shoulder as she guided him towards her garden gate. They had a lot of life to catch up on. "So, this is *your* place?! You know I had my heart set on buying this old place the moment I laid my eyes on it!" He looked half annoyed at the fact.

"Yes, I think I heard a little bird mention that," she responded with a sassy grin. "Come on Billy, I think we had better put a pot of coffee on for this catch-up." The two of them walked up the path and into the house. As always, Old Bill was sitting in the bay window, waiting expectantly. When Maggie opened the door, he greeted her affectionately, meowing his complaints of being alone and his cat-like desperation of hunger. She patted him on the head like usual and laughed as he suddenly noticed she wasn't alone. He stopped in his tracks and turned sideways, wondering who this new person was and why he hadn't smelled them before.

"Ah, now who's this?" asked Billy as he bent down to meet the curious feline. Maggie opened her mouth to answer, closed it again, and gave a little giggle. Billy looked up at her as the cat rubbed his face against Billy's hand.

"Billy, meet…Bill," she said, smiling sheepishly. Billy's eyes couldn't have smiled any brighter and his cheeky grin took over his whole face.

"Well now, that is a fine name for such a handsome fella. Nice to meet you, Mr. Bill," he winked at Maggie and then looked back down at Bill, gave him another pat, and stood up to follow Maggie into the kitchen. "Now, how ever did you come up with such a fine name Mag?" he asked mockingly, giving her shoulder a little rub as he passed her.

"Oh, it just sort of came to me," she answered, grinning playfully at him.

As the coffee was brewing, Maggie took him on a tour of her home. They were on their way back downstairs when Billy said, "I see why you called me for a hand. The place is beautiful Mag, but you're right, it does need a lot of TLC." Once the coffee was ready, they took their first cups out back to enjoy them in the quiet of the afternoon. She had a few cookies that she had baked earlier in the week and grabbed them so they had something to snack on. They got settled at her patio set, ready to catch up.

"I still can't believe you are sitting here! I actually thought I was hallucinating back at the shop," she laughed.

"That would explain the deer in the headlights look you were giving me," he laughed back. It felt so good to hear him laughing and to laugh with him again. They talked the rest of the day and well into the night. They remembered every detail of their week together so vividly. She couldn't believe how much he had retained. She, herself, had re-lived that week so often it was like a favourite, worn-out movie to her, but to know that he had too blew her mind. She told him about Pete, her ex-husband, the declining intimacy between them, his fading love for her, his infidelity, and the breaking down of their marriage. She spoke of how she knew it was never really meant to be anyway, but how rejection and betrayal had still been such a bitter pill to swallow. She spoke of the years that she had stayed on the farm, taking care of it and her parents, and not living for herself. She explained that she needed to live her own life, packed up, and left it all behind her, and ended up here. Billy shared the loss of his own parents a couple of years before moving to Jamaica, and how it took him a long time to work through that. That he had felt so much guilt not being around more and then how sudden their loss had been.

He told her of his years in military school, graduating and traveling all over the world, climbing his way up to Sergeant Major before receiving medical leave with honours. He had sustained an injury that caused some hearing loss that made his life, literally, quite dizzying. It had taken him some time to adjust and find his balance again, and fortunately, the off-balance effects did wear off quite a bit after a number of years; although, he retained some of the hearing loss. He spoke of how he was lucky his injuries hadn't been worse and that he was glad to be able to start working again, even though going back to the military was not in the cards. He had decided to move on and had been living in Jamaica for the past 10 years. He lived off his pension, making money doing odd jobs here and there, but after a time, he decided he needed to come back to the places he hadn't been since before he left for school. He had never married, except being married to his job of course. He shared how he had felt so lost when he was first dismissed. He had thought he'd stay in Jamaica until the end of his days but had felt such a tug to leave.

So, like her, he just packed up what he could carry on his bike, and with his guitar on his back, headed for the open road. No plan and no idea where he was going to end up. Only knowing something was pulling him and knowing that he just needed to follow his instincts. So, after months of driving and stopping, thinking each stop would be a fine place to end up but still feeling that pull to move on, he'd pack up again and climb back onto "his beast" to ride some more. Then one day he found himself in this tiny little town of Tamarack and thought it was as good a place as any to stop. He'd hoped to find a little place to buy. Unfortunately, there were no houses for sale, and after weeks of sleeping at the bed and breakfast, he couldn't stand another day with Pat and Stan.

"Not that they are horrible people or anything," he explained. "Quite the opposite actually. Couldn't do enough for me, but that was the problem. I started to feel like a little boy again with a mom that outdid the term 'mollycoddle' to the extreme. I think they've been bored for a while and a new face in town was just too much!" So off he'd gone. Heading, once again, out on the open road, hoping to find another place to settle.

But then about a week after leaving, he got a message. Maggie's message. He couldn't even begin to believe the odds and tried to talk himself out of hoping it could be "his Mag". He had already ridden another three days north after listening to her message and had been trying to ignore his curiosity when he finally decided to turn the bike around. He ended up riding straight through until he arrived back and found himself parked right outside Ashberry's Book Shop.

"How is it you were just down the street all that time, and we never ran into each other?" she asked him.

"Well, when I wasn't hiding out in my room, I was out riding the beast for days at a time, looking for a place to buy. Enjoying the open road again and feeling the wind in my sails. Guess our paths weren't meant to cross again until now, Mag." was his reply. "Although, when I first saw the sign on your shop, I thought about popping in. Lord knows I'd whispered the name 'Maggie Ashberry' to myself countless times over the years. But I figured, given the state of the other shop owners, that 'Ashberry Books' was probably owned by some old fart, and it was just the universe having a bit of fun with my tired heart."

She smiled at him tenderly, hardly believing that they were sitting with each other once again, and thinking to herself, *And now, here you are, against so many odds, back in my life.*

CHAPTER 7

Billy checked back into Pat and Stan's b and b the next day, indefinitely, although he spent most of his time at Maggie's. It felt just like old times again. Well, almost. They seemed to pick up right where they'd left off, except in one department. Maggie was holding back on reviving the intimate part of their history. It wasn't because she didn't think about it. Heaven knew she thought about it plenty. It wasn't because she didn't want to either. She just couldn't let herself take the plunge for some reason. They had a lifetime between them, and even with their past, she felt like they were strangers.

One evening, after working up on the porch roof together, the two of them took a break. Billy had his guitar with him and they sat singing some old favourites together, laughing and enjoying one another's company. Billy brought up that night long ago when the two of them went out in the snow to fix the hole in the cabin roof. As he spoke, she felt the familiar magnetic pull between them. Although it had been so long ago, the intensity between them was still beyond measure. As they walked over to the porch swing and sat down, Maggie thought she might just explode on the spot. Sitting there with him after all those years, hearing his husky voice, singing with him, and loving the harmony of their voices tangled together again. Smelling the hot spiciness of his skin, watching his movements, loving the twinkle in his eyes when he smiled at her, feeling his energy, and hearing him talk about their first night together was almost too much. She didn't know if she was going to spontaneously combust or find herself suddenly jumping his bones then and there on the front porch. He reached his hand out and slid it over top of hers, looking hungrily into her eyes. Maggie's heart started pounding as she looked back into Billy's eyes.

"I haven't seen that look in a long time, Billy," she said quietly, feeling like her body was floating. Before she could say anything else, he was sliding closer to her across the seat of the porch swing. His face was now inches away. She could feel his warm breath on her face and found herself quite weak with anticipation. She watched as he continued to draw closer, their eyes locked intensely, and watched as his lips gently parted. Their lips were nearly touching, Maggie's chest rising with arousal, her own lips now wet as she opened them slightly. She closed her eyes, feeling her skin tingle as his lips met hers, and they kissed slowly and deeply. It felt like they were one being. She didn't want to stop kissing him. The tenderness and electricity between them were stronger than she remembered.

Although she felt the urge to invite him upstairs, she stopped it, affectionately kissing his cheek and whispering in his ear, "I'm so glad you're here Billy. I think I must be dreaming." She stood up, still holding his hand. "I think we better call it a night. Tomorrow's my early day at the shop. You'll pop by for lunch, right?" she asked as he stood up and leaned down to kiss her forehead.

"Wouldn't miss it for the world." He gave her hand a little squeeze, letting go as he smiled and walked down the front steps towards the garden gate. As he was leaving, he called out "Pleasant dreams my dear

Mag," and she heard the gate swing shut.

They continued spending most of their days together. They worked on the outside of the house when she wasn't at the shop, and on the days she worked, he kept himself busy at odd jobs around town as well as doing his usual morning jog and short workout. Billy usually came by for lunch even if they didn't have work to do in her old house. They often found themselves singing as he played his guitar, fondly recalling the funny stories of their fellow cabin friends. He had even started going fishing with her and Carla on Mondays. Carla was over the moon for Maggie and had no problem "enjoy'n the scenery" as she put it. "Any chance to catch a glimpse of that 'good arse,'" was what she told Maggie. One particularly hot day, both she and Maggie got a great peek at that good arse. The three of them had been sitting under the willow for a couple of hours and had had a *few* bites, but the air had turned a bit muggy and was growing thicker, and the wind had completely stilled, so they were thinking about packing it in.

They were all feeling pretty hot when Billy chuckled to himself and turned to Maggie. "Hey Mag, remember that night at the cabin when we all went down to the hot springs for a skinny dip?" She giggled when she saw Carla perk up, ready for a juicy story.

"How could I forget? First and last time, actually, that I ever went skinny dipping. Goodness, that was a fun night wasn't it?" She felt her cheeks redden.

"Yes, it was Mag," he answered as he stood up, pulling his T-shirt over his head and dropping it on the ground next to her. She couldn't help but admire his body. Yes, like herself, the years had found their way to Billy. When she last laid eyes on him he still had his thin, soft, muscular, youthful body but she found a new attraction now. He was thicker and there was definitely more hair, some of which had started to whiten. But he was so tanned from working outside and he was still muscular and impressively firm. Just as she was thinking about how firm he still was, he tossed his jeans and headed down to the water, calling after her.

"Well, you can't go through life only skinny dipping once! Come on ladies, the last one in has to clean today's catches." Carla was already standing, smiling broadly at him as she watched him jog off.

"See Mags, what'd I tell you?! Good arse! Great arse!" Maggie stood up now too and gave Carla a little bump on the arm, laughing as she spoke.

"Hey, snap out of it Carla, you're drooling." Carla smiled back at her. "You're right though, that is one fine bottom! Always was!" Carla looked at her grinning.

"Well, better follow him, eh Mags?! Can't let the man skinny dip all on his lonesome now, can we?" Maggie suddenly felt like running in the opposite direction.

"I can't go skinny dipping! I'm almost, well, you know. I'm not what you could call young anymore." Carla turned around and looked Maggie straight in the eyes.

"Now you listen here, Ms. Maggie. You're still one fine catch, and that man down there thinks he'd like to skinny dip with you. All he's thinking about is that time you did, and he wants to relive some fond memories." Maggie felt her body droop on the spot.

"Well that's the problem right there, isn't it Carla? He remembers 18-year-old me. I don't look like her anymore. Plus, that last time was at night!" Just then they heard a splash and Billy calling up from the end of the dock.

"You ladies coming in or am I just a naked guy swimming alone?" They caught another glimpse of his firm bottom as he dove under the water and swam towards the middle of the lake. Carla was now stripped down to her bra and underwear and headed for the water.

"Come on Mags. I'll keep my unmentionables on so as not to outshine ya!" she joked and winked at her friend. "How 'bout you strip down and get yourself into that water before he's back at the dock?" And off she went. Maggie stood there for a moment, thinking about all the good reasons why she shouldn't do it. Then, just before Carla jumped in, she called back, "Thought you left the farm to do some livi'n Mags!" Maggie stood there for a few more seconds, then her next thought was that Carla had a point. If not now, when? She started towards the dock, peeling clothes off as she went. She stalled one last time before stripping right down to her birthday suit and jumping off the end of the dock. She'd forgotten how wonderful it felt to swim naked. There was nothing like it. So freeing and fantastic. Soon, the three of them were splashing and laughing like teenagers together. After a while, Carla made her way back to the dock to sit in the sun and dry her "unmentionables" off a bit. Maggie and Billy were still swimming and chatting about old times.

They were mostly laughing, remembering all the fun they had had that week long ago. But there came a moment when they stopped talking as they both trod water. Their eyes met, and she noticed he was looking at her differently. She wasn't really sure what it was, but she felt such a wave of affection, a longing for her, coming from him. They soon found themselves within a foot of each other's grasp, and she felt his hand brush against her arm. She was just able to touch the bottom of the lake now and was thinking of swimming back to the dock when she felt him reach out to her again, now pulling her towards him.

He had that twinkly, smiley-eye thing going on, and she felt her heart skip a beat. There they were, naked, body almost right against body. The water lapped teasingly in the spaces between them as they continued to tread. She wanted this moment to last. She wanted their bodies to become entangled so desperately but she felt resistance as well. She wanted to fight it and swim back to the dock but found herself happily lost in his eyes, the water moving their bodies together, apart, together.

"Maggie, you're still so beautiful." He pulled her a little closer. She smiled at him, and he kissed her softly. With their wet faces dripping in the lake, the two of them were lost amid old memories. "You always looked your most beautiful in the water," Billy said, his eyes smiling cheekily as he hesitated for a moment then added, "And right after we'd made love." Maggie felt her cheeks go red. They found themselves lost in one another's eyes. Staring deeply, Maggie could feel the electric energy building between them. She felt the urge to pull him tight and feel him deep inside. Snapping herself out of images of climbing on top of him, she held his face, kissed him softly, and then gently let go, smiling at him as she turned and swam towards the dock.

"Getting a bit too cooled off now; think I had better dry off a bit with Carla."

He smiled back. "Sure thing Mag, I'll join you soon." He gave her one of his cheeky grins and turned to swim away. She waited until he dove back under before climbing out and grabbing her clothes to join Carla. She decided she couldn't keep her story to herself anymore. So, before Billy was back, she spilled the beans.

"Hey Carla, do you remember me talking about my week at the cabin?" she asked her friend, grinning. Carla sat up and looked at Maggie questioningly.

"You mean your first time get'n lucky week? Ya, what about it?" Maggie hesitated and Carla spoke again. "You worried you're a newb again Mags?" she laughed.

"Very funny, but no. Do you remember the guy's name?" Carla was thinking hard and then her eyes widened.

"NOO!? That's a weird coincidence isn't it Mags?" Maggie laughed out loud.

"That's him, Carla! He's *my* Billy," she said, pointing over to the lake.

"Well shit Mags. I was wondering why you two had gone skinny dipping. Now you *gotta* clear the cobwebs for sure." Maggie rolled her eyes, thinking maybe she shouldn't have told her after all. Once they were all dressed and packed up, they headed back home. No one said much. Well, except for Carla's usual banter. Although, the sexual tension was a strong force within the cab of the truck. Maggie was sure she was glowing. Carla dropped Maggie off first, then she dropped Billy off at Pat and Stan's, sneaking another look at that "good arse" as he climbed out of her truck.

"See you later, thanks Carla," he called as the door swung shut.

"You bet, sweet cheeks," she called after him, and he chuckled to himself as he made his way inside the building.

Billy still hadn't had any luck buying a house, which wasn't surprising given that it was such a small town with not much of a turnaround with the locals. He didn't mind Pat and Stan's so much now that he had Maggie back in his life. He was really only at the b and b to sleep and didn't see Pat and Stan much, so he wasn't feeling overly coddled by Pat anymore. He was more than happy to be spending so much time with Maggie again. Things between them felt so much like they had all those years ago. Although they had history and spent almost every day together over the month, Maggie still hadn't let herself "fall" into anything serious with him. She also couldn't let go of the idea of becoming intimate, and then having him leave her.

All they had to build from was a week of youthful lust. She loved being with him, and she knew the attraction was still there. She wasn't really sure what was holding her back. Her worried, negative self-talk was running rampant again. What if he decided she wasn't for him after all? Maybe it was because she had gotten so good at being numb. Maybe it was because she had built such a tough shell around herself that she couldn't let him in. Maybe she still didn't believe in her own worthiness. Maybe she was just too old and out of practice, or maybe she was just scared of falling for him and losing him all over again. Still, their time together *was* amazing, and she knew, without a doubt, that the passion was still there, waiting to burst from within if she'd let it. For now, she continued to keep her intense feelings at bay. Instead, she enjoyed their reconnecting without benefits, as they say. Working on the house together. Talking and laughing like they'd always been together.

One night, after Billy had already been by for lunch and helped with putting up the new beams for the pergola, Maggie was sitting out back. She was enjoying the beginning of a beautiful sunset when she heard the now familiar, low grumble of Billy's motorcycle. She hadn't been expecting him until tomorrow but was pleasantly surprised that he was back. The gate swung open and there he stood in his jean jacket, an extra helmet tucked under one arm, looking good enough to eat.

"What do you say, Mag?" He flashed his sexiest smile at her and she felt her face flush, her heartbeat quickening. He was making his way towards her, still smiling, and said, "There's a full moon tonight, and I thought it would be a nice night for a ride." She sat there reluctantly for a moment, trying to think of an excuse to not say yes. It was as if she was trying to find a way not to let herself enjoy this moment. She shook herself from the "old Maggie" way of thinking and smiled. *Why shouldn't I go?* she thought to herself. Even after all these years, she was still experiencing first times and was loving every second, so why not add riding a motorcycle to the list? She stood up and smiled at him. He stepped close enough to reach out his hand for hers. She took it and they went into the house together.

"Do you think I should change, Billy?" she asked him, looking down at what she had on. She was still in the old T-shirt and jeans she had on from when they had been working on the beams earlier and her hair was in a messy braid running down one shoulder.

"No Mag, I wouldn't change a thing," was his response and she felt her knees go a little weak. "Maybe just grab a jacket; it gets pretty cool on the beast once I get her going." She grinned and grabbed an old leather jacket she hadn't worn in years from the new wardrobe. "Mmm," he said, looking her up and down as they walked out the front door and she strapped on her helmet. "This look suits you, Mag. Don't know if I'll be able to concentrate on the road." He took her hand in his and led her to his bike. He expertly straddled the bike and then nodded his head at her to hop on. She climbed up behind him and wrapped her arms around his waist. "You ready?" he asked.

"I think so," came her reply.

"You just keep holding on like that and let me know if you want to stop and come back home," he told her and kicked the beast into life. The robust, throaty growl was more than she anticipated.

"Holy shit!" she cried out, and he laughed and revved the engine. The sensation was unreal. *Wow*, she thought. *Never felt anything quite like this between my legs before*, and off they went. It was like nothing she'd ever known before. A freedom that you can't describe with any justice. One you just have to experience yourself to understand the unleashed power and complete lawlessness. It was a combination of exhilaration and fear mixed in with pure pleasure. They rode west, watching the sun drop in a fiery blaze, the trees whipping past them, and no cars in sight. Soon the full moon was the only light they had besides the bike's front light on the road, casting quick shadows across the pavement. It was so beautiful and liberating. She held him tight but found herself slowly relaxing and loving the experience, feeling less nervous by the second. When they rode for what must have been hours, he pulled off the road and turned down a dirt path that wound through some thick trees. They took the dirt road a little slower and soon came out into a clearing. Maggie looked up in awe. They were now far enough out of the tall dense trees, with the moon somewhere behind them, to be able to see the vibrant colours of the aurora borealis dancing across the sky. Billy turned off the engine.

"You alright?" he asked as he slid off the bike. He could now see her beautiful smile in the glow of the northern lights. He smiled back and reached out his hand to help her down.

"I'm with you, Billy. Of course I am," she replied. Then she looked back up at the sky. Her feet touched down on the gravel; she looked back up at him and said, "There's nowhere else I'd rather be and no one else I'd rather be with." Billy undid his helmet and took it off, resting it on his bike. Maggie took hers off too and set it down next to his. He grabbed her suddenly and pulled her to him.

"Same goes for me, Mag." Then he leaned down and kissed her. There, under a purple, green, and turquoise display of shimmering, breathtaking beauty, they kissed and held each other. Then, with their arms wrapped around each other's waists they watched with wonder. "It's too bad we missed so many years together Mag," he said as they watched in fascination. "Don't think there's been a day I didn't think of you though," he added, pulling her closer to him and resting his head on hers.

"I wish we hadn't lost all those years we could have been together too, Billy," she said in answer, squeezing him a little tighter.

After they watched for quite some time, he turned to her and said, "Stay right there." She smiled and nodded at him, wondering what he was up to. She turned around and could just make out his silhouette walking back to the bike. Then she turned back and looked up at the sky again. There were no words that could describe the magic dancing above. She felt Billy's hand touch her arm and she turned to look at him. He was holding something she couldn't really make out. Then, she saw him throw a blanket down on the ground next to her and sit on top of it. In true Billy fashion, he reached a hand up to help her down. She took his hand and sat on the blanket next to him.

"So, you had a whole master plan then?" she asked him with a serious tone. Maggie grinned at him and touched his arm.

"Well, sort of," he answered, smiling back. "I thought it would be nice to come out tonight because the moon is so full and bright but these lights are part of the universe's master plan, I think." He looked up, enjoying the view with a smile. He had another blanket that he reached for and swung over them, wrapping it around their shoulders. Maggie snuggled up to him, pulling the blanket a little tighter. Billy turned again and pulled a thermos out of what she thought looked like the basket that she had noticed on the back of the bike when she had gotten on earlier.

"Wow, what else are you hiding over there, Billy?" She was able to catch him smile and wink at her. He poured two cups of hot chocolate for them and handed Maggie one. "Thank you," she said, taking the cup and having a sip. They sat there enjoying their drinks, leaning shoulder to shoulder, watching the lights in silence for a little while. They were the brightest Maggie had ever seen. Vibrant, then soft, then suddenly bright and thick, moving slowly, and almost like clouds. Looking straight up into the dark star-speckled sky, the lights became thick sheets of colour, dancing gracefully in waving lines, stretching across the sky. Out in the open like that, it felt like the beams of colour would come right down and touch them. It was absolutely spellbinding and breathtaking.

They sat in complete awe, soaking it all up. Then Billy sat his cup down, took hers, and sat it down too. He turned to face her, both still snuggled under the blanket. The lights were playing across their faces like turquoise fairy dust. It lit up their faces with muted colours then went dark again. The only sound was nature itself -the wind gently rustling the trees, an owl in the distance, and the odd cricket far off in the woods. Billy reached up a hand and held the back of Maggie's head, gently pulling her face to his. And, there in the magic of the northern lights, sitting in nature together, surrounded by the woods and darkness, they kissed. It was surreal.

His hand softly ran through her hair as he kissed her. His thumb ran along her cheek, then his hand was on her neck and back into her hair. She had goosebumps but it wasn't from the coolness of the night. She moved her body closer to his, reached up, and held his face with both her hands. He inhaled deeply and kissed her with a little more pressure. She ran her fingers through his hair feeling her way back along his strong jawline. Then she cradled the back of his head again and softly trailed her fingers down his neck. She felt him shudder. Now they were kissing more passionately. Both his hands were holding her head, softly squeezing into her curls. Their kisses became deeper and more sensual with each moment that passed. Their lips were moving like waves, ebbing and flowing together. He slipped his tongue between her lips, then kissed her top lip followed by her bottom one, lingering for a moment and sucking on her bottom lip. She let her mouth fall open slightly as he softly ran his tongue along her lips. She pulled it in, sucking it. They pulled each other closer and Billy kissed her harder.

She felt his hands slide down her back. He had pulled her right against him, both of them kneeling now so that their bodies were tightly pressed against each other. Their hands slid all over one another, pulling each other tight as their kisses became deeper. His hands slid under her shirt, his touch so warm and tender. Maggie's fingers slid up his neck and into his hair. Moaning their pleasure out loud, their appetites grew and the energy was building. Kissing deeper still, they lost themselves in the moment. Maggie suddenly backed off as she felt things were going to go too far.

She eased back on the intensity of her kiss and pulled back from Billy slightly. They slowed down and found themselves back to the soft, slow kisses they had started with. Sitting back down, now hand in hand, he kissed her cheek, then her closed eyes, her forehead, her other cheek, her nose, and her lips. Her lips kissed his face as he moved around hers. Then they looked at each other and smiled. Billy wrapped his arm around her. She nestled into him, and they sat there for a while longer, watching the sky, quietly content.

Billy finally broke the silence by asking, "Should we head back Mag?" She nodded her head on his shoulder.

"Yes, I guess we better." They stood up together, and before picking up the blankets, thermos, and cups, and putting everything back into the basket, Billy leaned down and kissed her once more. With dreamy looks cast at each other, they gathered up their things and walked back to the bike, hand in hand. The ride back was just as exciting and beautiful, the magic of the lights still with them. Although they both would have enjoyed each other's company for the whole night, Maggie quickly stopped him before he got off the bike.

"Thanks for an amazing night, Billy. That was really…" She shivered a little and felt her whole body tingle. Then, grinning, continued "magical." He grinned back at her and gave her that intense look that made her weak in the knees. Maggie said, "I don't think I'll be going into the bookshop tomorrow. If you feel like dropping by, I'll be home all day." She stretched up and gave him a lingering kiss, just like the ones they had shared for hours when they would say goodnight to each other at the cabin. His hand gently tangled in her curls, holding the back of her head as their lips lingered. They held hands as long as they could until just their fingertips were touching before letting go. Maggie turned and walked toward the gate. She opened it, gave Billy a wave, and found her way into the house. She was sure she was floating. "Wow! That was awesome!" she kept saying to herself. She felt like she could run a marathon and found it very difficult to get to sleep!

CHAPTER 8

The days that followed seemed to make things grow more intense between them. The yearning and desire were almost trumping Maggie's apprehension about letting herself fall back into bed with him. She had become well-practiced in staying numb. And she found that, as long as they kept busy with the house, they were able to carry on spending time together without her letting her guard (or her clothes) down. She was finding it harder and harder though. Sometimes when Billy would come over to help with the house and they'd stop for a break, he'd pull out his guitar and start playing old songs, and she'd find the temptation to jump him overwhelming again. She was definitely a sucker for Billy and his guitar. "Killing Me Softly" would pop into her head and she'd have to take a deep breath to carry on, fighting off any thoughts of him playing *her* like his guitar. Maggie continued gently sending him on his way if things got too heated, Billy patiently backing off and seemingly happy to just soak up whatever she'd offer him of herself. Be that her time, her heart, or her body. It was more than clear that he wanted more, but he hadn't pushed her, and she found that that actually made it a little harder for her to back off! *Maybe that's his plan*, she thought to herself with a grin.

Billy had been coming over to Maggie's every day now, and they had become quite comfortable with each other. They had such ease and familiarity it was as if their 25 years apart never happened. But Maggie found herself still closing up and, in keeping with her plan to stay at first base, sending him away with just a kiss. This was also in an attempt to keep herself safe from any potential heartbreak.

A few weeks after their skinny dip with Carla, Maggie got a call in the middle of the night. Carla was talking so fast she could hardly understand her.

"Mags…Stu…He ain't breathing…Passed out." Maggie jumped out of bed and flipped the light on. Her training kicked in automatically, her old nurse role taking over.

"Carla, slow down, what happened?" She was already pulling on a pair of pants and grabbing a sweater, heading down the stairs as her friend took a couple of deep breaths and spoke again.

"Mags, Stu was going on about some of the guys he'd been drinking with at The Tipsy Turkey. They'd got into a brawl, and he came home right pissed off. I tried to calm him down and we ended up getting into one of our massive fights. Next thing I know, he's grabbing his arm, curling up on the floor, yelling about pain, and now he's not breathing!" She had started to get panicky again.

"Ok, Carla. Did you call the ambulance? What about Doctor Trent?" Carla was saying something to Stu like she was trying to wake him up. "Carla?" Maggie called out.

"No Mags, I didn't call Trent. He's like 107 years old." She answered with more panic in her voice, but Maggie was happy to hear her friend's usual blunt sarcasm and knew she had stopped her panicking - for a moment anyway. Maggie was now at the front door, putting on her boots. "I called emergency, they're sending the helicopter," Carla said.

Maggie took a deep breath and said, "Listen, I'm going to hang up now Carla, but I'm on my way. I'll be there in five minutes." She hung up and was out the door. When Maggie arrived, she found Carla sitting on the kitchen floor next to Stu. Maggie had learned first aid a long time ago when she was in college but, thankfully, had never had to use it before. She was worried she might not remember what to do but luckily, it all seemed to come back to her.

Because Stu had passed out and didn't seem to be breathing, she started CPR while Carla sat over them crying, "Come on Stu, don't leave me Stu." Maggie kept at it for a good five minutes, breathing into Stu's lungs and doing chest compressions,repeating until finally she felt Stu inhale suddenly. He still hadn't come around, but he was breathing again, and they were grateful to hear the helicopter above them now. Carla was beside herself. Maggie grabbed Carla's purse and threw the strap over her friend's head as they went out to meet the emergency crew.

"Can only take one extra," yelled one of the paramedics to Carla and Maggie as they went inside to get Stu.

"Go Carla, let me know what's happening when you can," said Maggie as she gave her friend a hug and watched her climb in after the stretcher. She watched them fly off and then went back into the house, turned off the lights, and locked up. She got back in her car and took a moment to breathe, then started up the engine and made her way back home. She ended up staying up the rest of the night, worried and unable to sleep, hoping Carla would call. She must have just started to drift off somewhere around dawn when the phone rang. Maggie was startled at the sound and grabbed the phone quickly.

"Hello?" she answered.

"Mags, it's me," she heard Carla's voice. It sounded much less panicked than it had a few hours ago. "Stu's going to be okay Mags. Lucky for him, you knew how to get'm breathing again. Gawd, don't know what I would have done without the old arsehole." She laughed with relief as she finished.

"Oh Carla, that's great." Maggie felt her body relax a little.

"Ya, sure is Mags. Gonna keep'm in here for a bit, do some tests and keep'm under observation, but they say he'll make it. Say Mags, do me a couple of favours would ya? Let them know at the grocers and the post office that I won't be working for a few days, and can you feed the animals tonight and tomorrow for me too?"

"Of course!" Maggie reassured her friend. "I'll head over and let them know later today, and don't worry about the animals," she continued.

"Thanks Mags. Oh, the doc's here, better go see what news he might have. Thanks again." Maggie hung up the phone. She sat there for a while, feeling the effects of the night's adrenalin and worry. She realized at that moment just how precious life really was, and it reminded her of just how quickly someone can be taken from your life. She picked the phone up and called Billy.

He answered groggily. "Hullo?" came his sleepy, raspy voice. She looked up at her clock and saw that it was only 5:15.

"Hiya Billy, it's me. Sorry to wake you." Maggie heard him clear his throat before he spoke again.

"You alright Mag?" he asked with panic in his voice.

"Ya, I'm alright, mind if I come over though?" she asked, almost crying with relief just from hearing his voice.

"Ya, sure, now? Yes, I'll meet you down in the diner in fifteen." She exhaled with relief.

"OK, see you soon," she responded. In a zombie-like state, she got up and went to the bathroom to brush her teeth and give her face a few cold splashes of water before walking over to the bed and breakfast. Billy was already waiting at a table for her. Of course, no one else was there; it was still not even six in the morning. He stood up and walked over to her and she fell into his arms. She just wanted to hug him. Nothing else mattered to her, and she was overwhelmed with gratitude to have him back in her life again. She filled him in on the excitement of the night and they sat there talking for a bit before he stood up, put an arm around her, and lifted her from the chair.

"Come on Mag, let me walk you home. You look exhausted." She let him guide her out to the street where he kept his arm around her, and she rested her head on his shoulder as he walked her home. He walked her all the way up to her bed, watched her climb in, and then tucked her in.

"Will you stay with me for a bit Billy?" she asked him as he gave her a kiss on the forehead.

"You bet." She reached out a hand to hold his. Maggie drifted off fairly quickly, and when she woke up, the sun was already high in the sky and Billy was no longer sitting beside her bed. She lay there for a moment, thinking about how sweet he was and how she wished he was still there. Then, she rolled over and realized he was next to her, on top of the covers, fast asleep. She smiled to herself at the sight of him there, lying in her bed next to her.

I could get used to this, she thought to herself. Maggie leaned over and gave him a soft kiss on the cheek and covered him with her comforter before getting up and heading downstairs. She curled up in the bay window with Old Bill, thinking about the wonderful man she'd been so lucky to have come back into her life. She patted her cat softly, listening to his quiet purr as she gazed dreamily out the window. Billy came down a little while later and she made them both coffee. She gave both the grocery store and the post office calls letting them know that Carla would be off for a few days. After she hung up, she grabbed the old Afghan off the back of the corner chair and took it over to the couch where Billy was sitting. They spent the rest of the day underneath it, cuddled up on the couch watching old movies, talking, and occasionally laughing at Old Bill who kept taking turns to snuggle with each of them, clearly unable to decide who was comfier.

The phone rang just before she was heading out to the Myers' farm to feed the animals. It was Carla letting her know that, so far, all Stu's tests were as good as could be expected. He had suffered a heart attack and they said he'd be staying for at least a week to recover. She also wondered if Maggie would come and get her in two days. Carla said she wanted to spend the following night with Stu as there were still some test results she wanted to wait for, and she had some questions for the Doctor. Billy said he'd drive the two of them over and they'd pick her up, no problem. Maggie was glad to have Billy offer to go with her. It was quite a long drive in the middle of nowhere, and Maggie was relieved as she didn't really know that part of the world very well. Now, even more than ever, she was glad to have Billy by her side. Seeing Carla so worried about losing Stu, and Stu being so close to leaving her, really made Maggie grateful to have Billy back in her life. Billy didn't mention that he too was relieved and more than happy to drive them so he wouldn't be worrying about her. They finished having a quick bite to eat.

Billy was getting ready to head back to the b and b when Maggie asked, "Feel like coming with me to feed the animals?" Billy grinned, eyes twinkling.

"Will I get to see you in your boots Mag?" She laughed.

"Sure. You can wear some too, funny boy," she answered.

"Oh, well then, how can I resist?" was his response, and they left for the farm. The experience was completely new for Billy, and Maggie couldn't resist having the odd giggle at him as he awkwardly maneuvered his way around the cows, pigs, and horses.

"Shit, Mag, I never realized just how big they really are!" he said, standing outside the pigpen as Maggie dumped feed into the trough. "That's a lot of bacon!" he laughed. She just shook her head and giggled. As they drew nearer to the cow shed, Maggie heard one of the cows mooing with some urgency. "What's that about?" Billy asked with some worry in his voice. They went in and Maggie approached the cow making the noise, running her hand along its side.

"I think she's just hurting from needing to be milked. Say, can you grab that stool and the bucket for me please?" Maggie asked, pointing to the corner of the shed where they were kept. Billy grabbed them and brought them over. "Thanks!" she said and placed the stool next to the cow, sliding the bucket underneath. Billy watched in amazement as Maggie laid her head against the cow, talking to her gently, and running her hand along her side, patting her. The cow seemed to calm a little. Then, Maggie started to milk her.

"Wow!" came Billy's surprised voice. "Would you look at that?" Maggie laughed and looked up, smiling at him. She milked for about 10 minutes, then got up, giving the cow another pat.

"Have a seat," she said to Billy, motioning to the stool. He just stood there, gaping at her.

"Why?" he asked. Maggie reached out a hand and pulled him over to sit on the stool.

"Because you're going to give this a go," she answered and patted him on the shoulders. She bent down and gave him a kiss on the top of his head.

"Nah, I don't think I can, Mag." She chuckled at his sudden lack of bravery.

"Nothing to it Billy!" He looked up at her with fear in his eyes and swallowed hard.

"Okay, what do I do?" She knelt beside him and gave the cow a pat, as it had started to moo again. Billy jumped a little. "What's wrong with her?"

"Well, I think she knows you're a newb!" Maggie answered, laughing. "And she just needs more milking, don't worry. Say something to her. Snuggle up to her a little and talk to her." Billy thought for sure she was pulling his leg and looked at her with apprehension. "No, for real," She smiled. "She's never met you before and wants to get a feel for you before you lay your hands on her." Maggie laughed a little and Billy grinned at her, relaxing a bit at the comic relief. He put his head against the cow awkwardly and spoke.

"OK now darling, I'm Billy and there's nothing to worry about." Maggie held in a giggle and coaxed him again reassuringly.

"Okay, grab on," she said, "Nope, right there, against her belly, there you go." Billy held on rather reluctantly. "Now, holding on at the base, squeeze with your thumb and first finger. Continue squeezing with your remaining fingers. Squeeze and pull down the milk." He looked up at her again like he wished the shed floor would swallow him up. Laughing, she said, "You've got this Billy. And once you get it, it's like riding a bicycle; you never forget." He tried again but nothing happened.

"See, not cut out for this Mag." Maggie smiled at him. "You sure I'm not hurting her?" he asked worriedly.

She laughed a bit again, "No, you're not hurting her, I promise. She'll hurt more if she's not milked. Now try again. Squeeze and pull a little stronger. Like you're trying to move the almost finished toothpaste from the end of the tube out." Then, she placed her hands on top of his, guiding him.

He tried a couple more times and then… "Hey! It worked!" he exclaimed suddenly, quite pleased with himself. Laughing, she went to walk away, and he reached out for her. "Where are you going Mag?" She stopped and grinned.

"Well, there are two other cows that need milking Billy!" She smiled at him, grabbed another stool and bucket, and sat herself down at the next one. It took them about an hour and a half to finish milking, and by that time Billy's "inner farm boy" was feeling much braver. They fed the cows and then went to the stable to feed the horses.

"We don't have to milk them now, do we?" he asked, winking at her and looking at the horses. She hugged him, laughing, and they finished up by feeding the chickens. Then, they went inside to clean up a little. "Well now, I can't quite believe I just did that!" Maggie laughed and gave him a big kiss.

"Well done, Billy! I'll make a farm boy out of you yet," she teased. They locked up, hopped into the car, and headed back to town. She dropped Billy off at the b and b, the two of them smiling away about their farm fun. Smelly and dirty, but happy, they kissed goodnight.

"See you in the morning, Beautiful," Billy said, giving her one last glance before climbing out of her car.

"See you later, handsome farm boy," she answered, and she drove home.

Maggie had the hatchback with some snacks and a thermos of coffee all ready to go when Billy arrived. "Morning Mag, all set?" He smiled and leaned down, giving her a kiss on the top of her head.

She smiled up at him and answered, "Morning Billy, yep, all set."

She handed him her keys, walked over to the passenger side, and opened the door. "Just need to swing by the farm to feed the animals," she said. Billy stood up straighter and looked at her suddenly. She laughed and said, "Don't worry, no milking this time." He relaxed a bit and climbed into the car.

They used overalls this time so they weren't as mucky for their trip to the hospital. It didn't take them long to get all the animals fed. Billy took the hay mixture to the cows himself and fed his new girlfriends. Maggie fed the horses and pigs, and then the two of them met up at the chicken coop and threw the chicken feed out for the hens. They were soon on their way. They had about a four-hour trek to the hospital and chatted all the way there. First talking about Stu's heart attack, Carla's worry, and the relief they all felt knowing that he would be okay. The conversation eventually moved on to their past and the things they'd both been up to for the last 25 years. Maggie asked him what it was like being in the military, and Billy said he enjoyed the routine and discipline and the ability to travel a bit, but that it had been rather lonely. After his basic training, he moved on to advanced training and then joined his unit. He remained for several years, before getting injured and being dismissed.

"It was a completely different life for me Mag. Wouldn't say I didn't like it, and luckily my injuries were not life-threatening, but I am glad to be away from it now. I didn't like not being there when I was first dismissed though. I didn't know what to do with myself," he said with a look of distress. "I got so used to the routine and structure of it. I felt lost and found my regular life quite hectic. So, I decided to go to Jamaica for a complete change of scenery from the life I'd been dropped back into." Maggie reached out and rubbed his arm gently.

"Sounds like it was hard adapting to regular life again. Did you get to go anywhere exciting before you left the military?" He chuckled.

"Exciting? Hmm, well, we didn't get much time to *enjoy* the places we went to, Mag. Not what I'd call exciting. Always training and working, but I saw some beautiful places along the way." He seemed to be lost in thought for a moment before he spoke again. "Jamaica was interesting though. Beautiful! So relaxed and easy-going, and oh Mag, you would have loved all the music. Always, anywhere I'd go, there was music. Funny, you probably wouldn't have recognized me out there. I had a little shack on the beach where I fixed up boats and cars and even bicycles for the locals, and some tourists too. I just let my hair grow out. I even had a scruffy beard," he chuckled to himself now. "I looked a bit like an old, worn-out sea captain after all my years there. I sure met some interesting people, though I kept to myself mostly. Think I was hiding; I wasn't sure who I was anymore. I did end up playing a couple of nights a week in one of the nearby bars for some extra cash. Just wanted the company, Mag. I'd sit up front with my guitar, playing all our old songs. Sometimes the barman and his wife would get a bunch of people together and we'd all be singing their local songs. Had some fun times. There was always something missing though. Thought about trying to contact you a fair few times Mag! But then I'd think it probably wasn't a good idea to suddenly pop into your happily married life." He laughed to himself, shaking his head a little, thinking about it. He looked at her more seriously, no longer laughing. His eyes watched her with deep love, then looked back out at the road ahead. "Damn, I've missed you, Maggie," he told her. Maggie's gaze was soft and caring as she looked back at him.

"Ha, happily married life! Didn't quite work out that way," Maggie replied. "I am glad you're here now. I've missed you too Billy." They smiled at each other lovingly.

"So how about you Mag, has anything exciting happened to you over the years?" he asked her.

"Hmmm," she thought. "Well, would you consider cleaning up muck every day exciting? How about getting up and out to the barn to milk the cows by 5 am? Or, maybe helping calves and colts being born is exciting?" She grinned at him.

"Sure, the miracle parts are exciting." Maggie flashed him a big smile. "And milking cows is pretty exciting," he added, winking at her. "Say, weren't you going to be a nurse Mag?" Billy asked after a moment of quiet.

Maggie smiled softly. "Yes. I went to nursing school, got my degree, and even worked for a couple of years at our doctor's office in town." Maggie took a deep breath before finishing. "I didn't end up practicing after that though. Well, not with pay. My mom fell ill shortly after that and I ended up taking care of her and running the house with my dad before he needed me as his nurse too." Billy reached his hand over and placed it on Maggie's.

"Sorry, Mag." He looked at her empathetically, then back out the window.

"Yeah, funny how life works out," she replied, looking at him with adoration and smiling. They were pretty well caught up by the time they picked Carla up and, of course, Carla did most of the talking on the way home. She had a good laugh when Maggie told her about making a farmer out of Billy.

"Say, did you two go for a ride, Mags?" Carla asked. Maggie looked at her quickly, shocked at Carla's bluntness but Carla didn't seem to be egging her on.

"What?" Maggie asked, seeing that Billy was smirking a little.

"Did you go for a ride Mags, on Black Beauty?" Maggie started breathing again and laughed at herself.

"Ohh, no, didn't get a chance, Carla." Carla gave her a funny look, not sure what she had missed.

"Maybe you should teach Sweet Cheeks, the farm boy here, how to ride Mags." Maggie and Billy snickered a little with juvenile giddiness. "Oh, you two are too much!" Carla said suddenly. "Now I get why you looked so worried when I asked you about going for a ride Mags! Gawd! Dirty minds!" She laughed too. "Ever been on a horse, Billy Boy?" Carla asked him, still grinning.

"No, not something I've ever had the chance to try," Billy answered.

Maggie looked at him, smiling with hopefulness, saying, "Guess that will be your next farm lesson." Billy glanced at her, eyes twinkling cheekily, then looked back at the road with a grin as he answered.

"Sure Mag, I'd love a riding lesson from you." She felt her face go red and Carla let out a knowing laugh in the back.

"Okay you two, get a room." It had turned out to be a great road trip. Maggie was so glad that they had made the trip together.

CHAPTER 9

Maggie woke up wishing she didn't have to get out of bed. The trip to pick up Carla had been fun, but she felt like she could use some extra sleep. She laid there for a while, then dragged herself out of bed and got ready to face the day. She *had* to go to work today. She couldn't miss going in as she had decided to let some local groups use the book nook for gatherings and activities, and today was the day for her first group. So far it was just the lady's knit and crochet club who were having their first meeting that afternoon. She had a quick shower and opened the shop with an extra-large coffee in hand. The day passed slowly, and Maggie ended up reading for most of it. She had just managed to finish organizing the book nook and popping the kettle on when her group of "oldies" started filing in. She had a little kitchenette at the shop, so she told them she would accept a weekly donation and would make sure to have tea and cake or biscuits ready for their meetings. They would only be there from 2:00-4:30 on Tuesdays, and Maggie thought it might be kind of nice to have company and chatter as she worked around the shop. As they were ambling in, Billy popped by, smiling at and acknowledging the women who had arrived so far.

On his way past, he said, "Ladies," and gave them a wink before arriving at the counter to see Maggie. "Hey Mag, what's all this?" he asked, nodding his head towards the group.

"Oh, hiya Billy," she said with her big smile. "That's the local knit and crochet group. They're going to start using the nook every Tuesday instead of shifting between each other's houses. Thought I'd give them a break from their husbands," she said with a sassy smile.

"Oh, I see!" Billy grinned back. "What time are you done tonight?" He leaned over the counter, and she leaned to meet him halfway. They kissed each other on the cheeks.

"Oh, I should be on my way home just after five, I'm hoping. As long as I can shift this lot successfully," she replied, looking over at the old ladies now deciding whose spot was who's according to bathroom and exit needs. Billy laughed playfully. "Why, what's up?" she asked him.

"Oh, just thought I might pop by later. I missed having lunch together today." She was busy piling the teacups and biscuits onto a tray as he spoke. "Found myself daydreaming about old times." He added, his eyes dark and dreamy.

"Sure, sounds good Billy; probably safe to say I'll be home any time after 5:30." Billy nodded with his cheeky smile and headed out of the shop. "Evening, ladies," he called, earning a few giggles and happy smiles as he left the shop. Maggie grinned at how cute she thought he was as she carried the first tray over and sat it on the center table for the women. As she turned to go back for the other tray, one of the women stopped her, smiling up at her.

"You know dear, that fellow is awfully handsome and very polite." Maggie grinned back at her, nodding her agreement. "I think he's pretty sweet on you," the woman added with a little giggle. Maggie felt her body go warm and smiled again.

"Oh, you think so?" she replied, and the woman nodded up at her.

"Take it from an old, experienced lady dear - he's smitten." She was nodding her head faster and more purposefully at Maggie now. "If I were you, I'd grab'em while he's still a free man! You don't get many good ones like him anymore."

"Well, that's lovely, thank you." was all Maggie could think of saying. She smiled at the woman again before turning and walking over to the counter for the other tray and leaving it on the table next to the first one. She realized she was wearing a goofy dreamy expression and snapped herself out of it as she set to work again.

Encouraging the ladies to finish up at about 4:15, Maggie realized quickly that she'd have to start closer to 4:00 next time if she was going to get out by 5:00. They all, of course, had to use the bathroom before heading out, and between eight slow moving old women and one bathroom, that did take some time! They chatted all the way out the door as Maggie locked up behind them. It was getting quite dark for so early in the evening, and when Maggie looked up at the sky, she noticed some big, dark clouds that seemed to promise a good rainstorm. She said goodbye to the group, saying she'd see them next Tuesday, and they thanked her for the space and snacks, and off she went.

She arrived home just after 5:00, and when she opened her door, she was surprised not to have her usual greeting from Old Bill. She thought at first, *Maybe he's sleeping upstairs,* but he usually knew when she was coming, and he always heard the front garden gate. She shut the door, thinking that might get him running, but was starting to feel a little worried when there was still no Bill trotting towards her. She headed towards the kitchen and realized she could see lights flickering and hear music playing. As she came around the corner, there was Old

Bill, stretched out and fast asleep on the kitchen island. She had to try to keep from laughing out loud at what she saw next. There, in one of her frilly aprons, singing and dancing along to Barry White's "Can't Get Enough of Your Love" was Billy, working away in the kitchen with his back to her. He had the table set with candles and a bottle of what looked like champagne. She stepped back a little, hoping to watch a little more of the show before being found. She bit her lip, stifling a giggle as Billy slid his feet along the floor, singing into a wooden spoon, and every once in a while giving his hips a little shake. Reaching the climax of the song, he spun around, singing at the top of his lungs, and saw Maggie standing there trying not to laugh. He stopped dead in his tracks, still holding the wooden spoon up, looking a little bashful and very cute in her apron, his mouth hanging open slightly.

"Hi Billy," she said with a big grin. "Don't know if I should report a break-in and apron theft or not." She laughed out loud now and walked towards him. He grinned sheepishly as she came closer. "You look pretty cute in that apron, especially when you're shaking those sweet cheeks around." She laughed harder and saw his face go a little red.

"Didn't hear you come in Mag," he said, walking over and turning the radio down. Old Bill sat up and meowed at Maggie. She reached out and gave him a pat on the head, then leaned down and rubbed her face on the top of his furry head. Billy smiled, watching her loving her pet. "How are the happy old hookers?" he asked, grinning widely.

"Funny!" she answered. "Happily hooking, of course," she said, making a kind of "ha ha" gesture at his joke. He shrugged his shoulders a little and laughed. "So, what are you two boys up to then?" she asked inquiringly, looking from Old Bill to Billy.

"Carla lent me her key so I could surprise you with dinner," Bill answered, and he pointed towards the set table.

"Oh, very nice," she said and walked up to him, stood on the tips of her toes, and gave him a kiss. "Well, I'll let you boys carry on and go change out of my working girl's clothes." Maggie turned and walked away, still grinning broadly and laughing at the sheer cuteness of his unexpected appearance.

She changed out of her day's tank top and jeans and picked out a long summer dress. Then she grabbed her favourite little green sweater that matched her eyes and put that on too. When she got back downstairs, Billy was standing at the stove, radio turned back up, singing to Blue Rodeo's "Lost Together". It was much less comical and quite sexy, actually. Well, apart from the apron. She stopped and listened for a moment, loving hearing him sing along to one of her favourite bands. This time, when he heard her, he wasn't taken by embarrassed surprise and had a rather pleasant look of affection on his face.

"You clean up nice Mag," he said to her. She smiled and looked around, noticing that he had lit a few more candles and set them here and there on the counter and on the end of the island. They were casting a cozy golden glow on the walls around them. Billy turned the stove off and walked over to the other side of the island across from her. He stopped and looked at her, his eyes smiling in the flickering light. He was wearing some nice, butt-hugging jeans and had a white button-up T-shirt on. He looked incredibly handsome and Maggie found her pulse quickening with her attraction to him. He was also still wearing her apron, and she giggled again as he stood in front of her. He leaned across the island, reached out one hand, and held it softly against the side of her face. She looked down and he lifted her chin back up tenderly. "More and more beautiful each time I see you." He leaned a little closer and gave her a soft kiss.

As he stood back up, she walked around the counter toward him.

She smiled impishly and reached her arms around his waist and undid the apron. Billy grinned at her and pulled the strap over his head, placing the apron down on the counter. Maggie had her back to the island, and he moved towards her, lifting her off the floor. He sat her up on the island, leaning his hands down on either side of her on the countertop, looking deeply into her eyes.

She said, "You look rather scrumptious tonight, Billy," grabbing onto his shirt and pulling him close enough to kiss him. Every time they kissed, she felt herself lift off the Earth. A weightless, ethereal lightness she had never felt with anyone else. His hands came up to hold her face. They were so big she could feel his fingertips stretching out and tickling her hairline behind her ears. Their lips softly broke apart and he smiled down at her. It took everything in her not to wrap her legs around him and attack him.

"So, what'd you make me?" he asked her. She looked at him, confused.

"What did I make you? You're the one that broke in to make me dinner," she answered. He kissed her nose softly.

"No, I mean what did you make me - a scarf, some slippers?" Maggie kissed his chin.

"Oh, sorry, I'm not part of the club." He gave a little chuckle.

"Oh, I see. Well, what did the old hookers make me then?" She laughed at his joke, and he kissed her forehead.

"Well, they were pretty busy with their work, so I think you'll have to put in any requests you might have for anything in particular. Maybe I could ask them to make you an apron." He threw his head back with a chuckle, then kissed her on the end of her nose again. "Say, dinner smells really good Billy, when's it ready?" Maggie asked. He turned a little and gestured to the table.

"Well, whenever you are M'lady." He turned back and grabbed her waist to help her down.

"Excellent!" she smiled and headed for the table. Just then they heard the rain start coming down. Pouring down, hard and fast. Then, a bang that made them both jump a little, echoed through the room. The lights in the living room and hallway flickered, eventually going out. Everything was suddenly still except for the sound of the rain. Luckily, they already had candles lit, so they continued over to the table and sat down. "So, what's the occasion?" she asked him, looking deeply into those dark eyes of his.

"Just feeling lucky to have you in my life," he answered with his cheeky grin. "Damn, you really are beautiful." He stopped talking for a moment just staring at her. "This time together has been really special to me Mag." She reached out and took his hand.

"Me too Billy." They smiled at one another for a moment, then Billy reached out for the bottle on the table and motioned questioningly to her. He knew she wasn't a big drinker, but he also remembered her liking the champagne a few of them had sprung for one night at the cabin. She smiled and nodded, sliding their glasses over for him. After he poured two glasses, he went back into the kitchen and brought back their meals. He had made fettuccine for them with a big green salad on the side. They started eating and found they were staring at each other more than talking. Grinning with goofy smirks, eventually moving to hold hands and wiggle their fingers in and around each other. Their feet found their way to playing footsies under the table. After dinner, Billy held out a hand as he stood up. Maggie accepted it and let him lead her out to the back patio. He stood behind her and wrapped his arms around her, hugging her. They stood for the longest time, just watching and listening to the rain.

"That was delicious, thank you for dinner Billy." He hugged her even closer to him. She knew he probably wanted to suggest what they might do while the power was out since they couldn't watch TV or listen to the radio without it. Before he could bring it up, she suggested they find a board game to play. With one little flashlight, they went hunting, and finally, in a closet by the stairs, they managed to find Checkers, Monopoly, and Scrabble. Neither of them fancied Monopoly but they laughed when Maggie jokingly suggested strip Scrabble.

"Ha, you're on!" Billy answered quickly, and they went back to the kitchen to clear off the table and set up their game. Maggie said she'd be right back and carefully ran upstairs with the flashlight. She went to her room, threw on a pair of pants under her dress, a pair of socks, and another sweater and went back downstairs. "Hey, you can't do that Mag," he said, with a disappointed look on his face as she sat down at the table.

"My house, my Scrabble, my rules," she answered back with a playful smile.

"Fine," he answered. "But you're still going to lose Mag." She laughed. They laughed so much together. She had missed it so much. Billy won the start position and placed his first word - BUXOM.

"Wow," Maggie said, "You're getting right into the strip Scrabble theme, aren't you Billy?" She moved her tiles around and around, deciding she had crap letters and worrying a bit because their deal was five tiles or more per word, or something came off. Then she saw one, MEOWS, and placed it as her first word. They each picked five more tiles and tried for their next two words. By their fourth turn, Maggie was down one sweater. By their fifth, she was down a sock and so was Billy. They laughed and reached out, touching each other, sneaking in kisses here and there as they played. On turn eight, Maggie lost the other sock, and then she lost her other sweater. Billy was still out just one sock. They refilled their glasses and grew giddier with each round. Luckily for Maggie, the champagne seemed to make it hard for Billy to concentrate. By turn 12, he'd gone from leading to being out his other sock, his shirt, and his pants too. All he had left was his T-shirt and underwear. She didn't mind one bit.

"Not at all hard on the eyes," she said, reaching over and giving his leg a little rub, then sneaking in a kiss before placing her next word, JUICY. He grinned at her word and grinned even bigger when he placed his own down, NIBBLE. Maggie was now starting to sweat a little. This was partly because of the champagne and the almost naked man sitting across from her, but mostly because she had crappy letters again, and was worrying she'd be the one sitting there naked. For the next three turns, she wasn't able to get any words with five letters, and she was now down to her undies, pants, and bra.

"Loving this game, Mag! Never knew Scrabble could be so educational," he winked at her and leaned in for a lingering kiss. They both managed to get their next two words before Billy was down to just his underwear and Maggie in hers and her bra. They had finished off the champagne when the lights flicked back on, and the radio was playing again. Billy stood up and grabbed her hand, pulling her up and away from the table. He danced her around to "Runaround Sue" before they landed in a laughing heap on the couch. Maggie was not used to drinking so much, and Billy wasn't used to the effect champagne had on him. They ended up kissing each other to sleep right there in their undies with the unfinished game of Scrabble on the table.

They woke up together the next morning, cuddled up on the couch, still in their undies, both of them feeling a bit hungover from the champagne and late-night Scrabble. Maggie got up and got the coffee brewing right away then went up to shower before Billy roused too much. When she came back down, she grabbed herself a coffee and noticed Billy was up and had gone out back with his coffee, watching the sun starting to brighten up the tops of the trees.

"Morning Mag," he said with a sleepy smile as she went over and gave him a kiss then sat down in a chair next to him. "Fun night, eh?" he said, looking over at her and grinning.

"Yes!" she laughed. "What I remember of it," she added. She took another big sip of her coffee and swallowed. Billy's grin broadened, thinking about their game of Scrabble.

"Better get myself cleaned up, I guess. Mind if I use your shower?" She grinned amorously at the thought, then caught herself.

"Oh, sure, of course you can." As he walked inside, she called back, "Clean towels in the cupboard. Oh, and the shower takes a couple of flicks before it works, Billy." She hadn't realized he had popped his head back outside and she jumped a little when he spoke.

"OK Mag. I'll call you to come help me in there if I need you." Then he winked and walked off again.

CHAPTER 10

A couple of days after Carla got home, she stopped in at Ashberry Books to drop off some mail and say hello. Maggie was happy to see her friend stepping right back into being her usual, energetic, busy self. "Glad everything turned out alright Carla," Maggie said, smiling. "Are you still coming apple picking Friday?" she asked hopefully.

"Ah, I dunno Mags. What if the hospital calls? I was thinking I should head back there." Maggie gave her friend a little grin.

"I know you're still worried, but he's well taken care of. You could use a break from worrying about Stu and get off the farm for a few hours."

Carla thought about it for a moment, then answered, "Ya, yer probably right Mags. Say, is Billy coming?" Maggie was glad her friend had agreed.

"Oh, I haven't asked him," she answered. "He might want to come. I'll check with him when I see him later." Just then, a customer came in and Carla waved goodbye, heading out the door.

After a good day and a decent amount of books sold, Maggie packed up her things and headed home.

"Sure, sounds like good exercise," was Billy's response when she asked him over dinner that night. Maggie laughed.

"It is good exercise. Bet you'll be surprised how sore you are." He smiled back.

"Oh, I don't know. I'm pretty tough, Mag." He flashed his usual, flirty wink at her.

Carla had said she'd pick them up outside the bed and breakfast on Friday morning. Maggie decided to walk over and meet Billy for coffee while they waited for Carla. She walked into the b and b restaurant and saw him in his usual corner. Pat came over and said good morning, chatted a bit with them after pouring their coffees, and then left them to themselves with a happy look on her face. Billy was still feeling confident about not feeling the pains of apple picking. Maggie giggled, knowing he was in for a surprise.

Pulling up in her old truck, Carla gave a couple of honks. Maggie and Billy finished their coffees, said goodbye to Pat, and went out and climbed into the truck with big smiles on their faces.

"Morning you two," Carla said happily. "Glad you convinced me to come, Mags. You were right, better than sitting around worrying." She gave Maggie's hand a little pat as they drove out of town. They headed for Preston's Apple Orchard about four miles south of town and saw a number of other trucks already parked there as they pulled up. It was a breezy, sunny morning, a lovely day to be outside in the orchard, and the smell was intoxicating. They all went to the barn and got their baskets from Mrs. Preston, and Carla went back and grabbed the step ladder she had in the back of the pick-up. The three of them headed into the orchard, chatting away.

"You'll have to get Mags to bake you her famous apple crisp, Billy," Carla teased, looking up at Billy who was on the ladder, reaching for some of the nicest apples.

"Oh?" he said questioningly, looking down at them with a smile.

"Oh, shut up Carla!" Maggie said with some embarrassment. "It only happened once!" Carla was laughing now.

"What are you two talking about?" Billy asked. Maggie looked quickly at Carla, tilting her head a little, like she was trying to say "gimme a break." Carla laughed again.

"Well, ya see Sweet Cheeks, when Maggie first moved here around this time last year, I had convinced her to come out with me apple picking. She didn't have her house yet and was staying where you are now, so after we picked apples all day she said she wanted to make her famous apple crisp for Stu and I but couldn't make it at Pat and Stan's." Carla was still laughing. Maggie just stood there watching Billy look back and forth between the two of them, listening. "So, she got busy in our kitchen, proud as a peacock with her crisp. She threw it in the oven and went into the den to relax with Stu. I went out to feed the cows and horses, see, and Stu was already pickled, nicely dozing in his chair. Apparently, Mags here, worn out from her first-time apple pick'n, fell asleep too. The next thing I knew, there was black smoke come'n outta the kitchen window, smoke alarm blasting. Stu was running into the yard cursing and swearing 'What an effing way to wake up!' and Mags was almost in tears." Billy had joined in the laughter now.

Maggie was not impressed at all at the two of them laughing at her and was eagerly awaiting the end of Carla's story. "So, I ran into the kitchen and saw the smoke come'n outta the oven, grabbed the extinguisher off the wall, and blasted the stove good. After the fire was out and some of the smoke cleared, Stu went over to the oven and pulled out Mag's famous apple crisp. Well, it was crisp alright!" Carla was holding her belly to keep from laughing. "Stu plunked it down on top of the stove and said, 'Your crisp is done, Maggie.' Then he walked back to the living room, a hand waving through the smoke, and sat back in his chair." Billy was laughing harder now too as he climbed down the ladder and joined them. He looked at Maggie, tried to stop himself from laughing and reached out a hand apologetically. Maggie looked at him and Carla, trying to keep a look of seriousness on her face, but couldn't help but laugh along with them. "So, now Mags isn't allowed near our stove when she comes over. Stu's house rule," Carla added with one last laugh. Then, she suddenly went quiet. "Damn glad you do first aid better than you bake apple crisp, Mags." After a moment of serious silence, the three of them started laughing again.

They managed to pick three bushels before calling it a day. Billy and Maggie had decided to share one bushel between the two of them and Carla claimed the other two. "Stu'll be happier than a pig'n'shit," Carla said on their way back home.

"Fond of apples, is he Carla?" asked Billy.

She snorted a reply, "More like fond of cider."

He grinned and Maggie heard him say, under his breath, "Might have known." They were all sweaty and worn out, and Maggie didn't feel much like making dinner. Carla dropped them off in front of Maggie's house, eager to get herself back and get her chores done in case the hospital called. She drove off with a beep of her horn. Billy suggested they get cleaned up, and he'd get them a bite to eat at the bed and breakfast.

"Sounds like a plan," Maggie responded. "I'll meet you back at Pat and Stan's in about half an hour." He bent down and gave her a kiss, and as he did, he made a little grunting noise. "You okay Billy?" She laughed a little when she asked, knowing he was already feeling the aches and pains from his first time apple picking.

"Oh, yeah, just fine," he answered, trying to stand up without grimacing. She grinned at him again and headed towards the house.

"See you in a bit, Billy."

"Yep, see you soon." Maggie turned around to watch him walking away. He was moving a little slower than usual, and she grinned as she watched, enjoying the view immensely.

They met back at the bed and breakfast and found the table in the corner free. Billy pulled a chair out for Maggie, then sat across from her. There were a few other tables occupied, but not too many people. Just enough to keep Pat happily busy. She was chatting with an older couple at a table nearby when she saw Maggie and Billy sit down and came over to get their orders. As they sat there together, waiting for their dinner, Maggie looked at Billy and knew he was already sore. She could already feel it in her own shoulders. He tried not to let on just how much, though. They ate well, having worked up a good appetite from their day's work. After they finished their dinner, they even got a piece of pie to share. They took small spoonfuls, peeking up into one another's eyes as they ate, grinning as their feet rubbed together under the table teasingly. Maggie left the last mouthful for Billy. He looked intensely into her eyes as he enjoyed his last bite. His eyes twinkled mischievously as he soaked her up.

After they finished their cups of coffee, Billy promptly got up. "Be right back Mag," he said. He walked over to Pat and spoke to her quietly for a moment, then came back wearing his cheeky grin and sat down again.

"What's that about?" she asked him.

"Oh, nothing much. Pat asked me the other day if I could do some work for them while I'm staying here, so I was just letting her know when I was available." Maggie had a feeling he wasn't telling the whole truth but didn't press. She saw Pat walk over to the register counter and play around with the radio for a moment. She then turned it up enough for them to hear the music. A song was just ending and a slower one came on. It was one she hadn't heard for a very long time. She smiled, remembering it fondly, then noticed Billy standing up again.

She started to ask, "Where are you going now?" Then he was standing in front of her with his hand out.

"Care for this dance?" He grinned his Billy grin at her again. She smiled back and looked around as she took his hand and stood up. All eyes were on them, even Pat and her young helper had stopped to gawk. He led her out into an open area of the floor, still holding her hand, and placed the other on the small of her back, pulling her close and moving them to the music. She rested her free hand on his shoulder. The song playing was "Never Tear Us Apart," which Maggie thought was quite fitting for them and brought back numerous memories. He placed her other hand up on his shoulder and wrapped both of his around her lower back. At first, Maggie was still aware of the eyes on them, but soon, she drifted into feeling like it was just the two of them. Maggie felt the universe fading around them.

They had only had that week together all those years ago, but they had danced so much. One of the many songs was this one. It was a big deal around that time and played on the radio often. Maggie had always loved dancing and she remembered how she used to go out with her girlfriends. There was always a hockey or baseball dance at the end of the seasons, and there was often someone getting married, and having a Buck and Doe, so she went dancing fairly often growing up. Then there was all the dancing she and Billy had done, and she thought about how much she had missed listening to him play his guitar and sing to her too. Her memories of them were surrounded by so much music in their short days with one another. He was a good dancer and she loved how he took the lead and moved her around the floor. Singing in her ear here and there, not able to help himself, being such a lover of music too. Her arms still draped around his neck, her head resting on his chest, his arms totally enveloping her in his embrace, his hands falling just past her waist, his head resting on hers, they rocked back and forth. They were enjoying being the only ones on Earth for a few minutes in time. Feeling like they did as teenagers with not a care in the world. Just them, their love of music, and their love for each other.

As the song ended, he dipped her slightly and brought her back up against him. She giggled a little hearing him grunt a bit from his sore, apple picking muscles. As they stopped dancing, still holding each other, Billy smiled down at her and kissed her on the end of her nose. Maggie grinned and then heard the older couple near their table call out "Encore!" and she turned to see them, and Pat, clapping. Maggie and Billy smiled at them politely, then walked over to the counter where Billy paid the bill, thanking Pat. The two of them left the b and b and stepped out into the fresh evening air. Maggie invited him back to her place for a nightcap - this for Maggie usually meant a cup of tea, but she knew she still had a few beers in the fridge if Billy preferred that. As they walked hand in hand, Billy finally admitted to apple picking defeat and Maggie had a good laugh.

"I told you you'd be hurting! You just wait till tomorrow, Billy!" She gave him a little slap on the butt.

He jumped a little, and involuntarily gave a little "Ow." She linked her arm through his and they leaned on each other the rest of the way. "I really didn't expect to feel it so much Mag! All the things I do fixing stuff! Up and down ladders and carrying things all the time." She thought he looked so cute as he tried to be his usual, strong, invincible-man, self.

"Well, you used different muscles keeping your arms above your head like that, plucking apples for all those hours," Maggie responded as she gave his shoulders a little rub on their way up her porch steps. "How about I give you a nice rub down with some coconut oil and lavender?" He turned and looked at her and she saw a little twinkle in his eye.

"Oh, would you Mag? That sounds perfect." She laughed again as they went into the house. Old Bill came trotting towards them, happy they were back and more than ready for some rubs of his own.

Maggie sat Billy down on the big ottoman at the end of Carla's favourite chair and stood behind him with the oils in hand as he pulled his shirt over his head. He was so tanned, and his shoulders were so thick and broad. Maggie had a sudden urge to lean down and smell him, maybe even give him a little nibble. *Maggie, snap out of it,* she thought to herself and proceeded to drop some lavender into her hands and then rub the coconut oil onto his back. He shivered a little at the coolness of the coconut oil, but as soon as Maggie started to distribute an equal amount across his shoulder blades, he leaned back slightly into her hands, and she heard him give a satisfied moan as she felt his body relax. His skin was so smooth, and as she massaged the oils into his muscles, she found herself fantasizing again.

As she rubbed into his shoulders, his neck, and down the center of his back, all she could see was herself stripping down and pressing her naked body to his, skin to skin over his back. As she continued to knead and squeeze his tight muscles, she found her face getting closer and closer to his neck and imagining herself kissing and licking her way up and down his body. She was awakened from her tantalizing thoughts by Old Bill's sudden arrival and howl from the chair behind her. She pulled away from Billy a little, then gave his back one last rub before finishing, letting her hand slide across his shoulders as she walked around to face him. He opened his eyes and looked up at her.

"Gawd, thanks Mag. That felt really good." He grabbed onto her dress belt and pulled her in, sitting her down on his lap so that she was straddling him. He rested his face against her chest, and she wrapped her arms around his neck softly as he nuzzled his head into her body. She gently ran her fingers through his hair. It was still fairly dark with the odd streak of silver woven into it. Maggie was sorry they hadn't grown older, together during those changes. He was somehow even more attractive than when they were younger. She pulled him in a little tighter and then lifted his chin up gently, leaning her face down and kissing him tenderly. Billy looked up into her emerald green eyes with a sexy grin, his eyes twinkling. "Hey Mag, remember that time on the bus?" he asked her, smiling even more now. She felt her skin flush and smiled back at him.

"Oh, my gawd Billy! I've re-lived that moment far too many times in my mind." He kissed her again. His hands were resting above her bottom, and she felt him stretch out his hands wide and pull her closer still, both lost in the memory as their lips lingered on each other. The group at the cabin had rented a beat-up, old bus to use while they were there. It was big enough for all of them to go out for day trips if they wanted, and on one of the trips they made, Maggie and Billy had snuck away from the rest of the group and gone back to the bus on their own. The bus was parked off a dirt road, under some trees in a sort of field driveway.

They went inside and, making their way to the back, found they were quite hidden and secluded. Billy sat down in the very back seat and Maggie climbed right on top of him. It all happened so quickly and heatedly. He undid his pants and pulled them down just enough for her to get to him. She pulled her underwear off, lifted her long skirt, and sat down again, letting him slide right in and taking him in all the way. She grabbed the back of the bus seat behind his head. He held her hips and helped her glide up and down, then in a rush of pure pleasure, they were both screaming their satisfaction within moments. It was fast, effective, and delicious. They got themselves fixed up and headed back to where everyone was meeting up, both grinning happily.

Her heart was racing again thinking about it, and now, here they were again. Maggie straddled atop Billy in a snug embrace. Their lips unlocked and she smiled at him. They looked at each other intensely for a few seconds, then she started to climb off him. She could feel how hard he was and felt quite hot and amorous herself.

As she stood in front of him, she asked, "Feel like a brew or maybe a cold one?"

He hesitated for a moment, still holding onto her as she stood there. He looked like he wanted to say something but stopped himself, then answered with, "Better make it a cold one." As she started to walk away, Billy pulled her back, grabbing both her hands. He looked up into her eyes and said, "Say Mag, there's something I have to know."

Maggie suddenly felt a little uneasy at his seriousness, but smiled and said, "Sure Billy." He hesitated, looking down, then lifted his head back up. She realized his eyes were full of sadness.

"Am I wasting my time here?" She felt herself harden and suddenly felt the need to put up her defenses. Billy sensed her walls going up and continued. "What I mean is, it seems like every time we get, you know, close, you push me away, and I don't want to do anything to hurt you, Mag. I won't do anything at all if you don't want me to. But I gotta know… do you not find me attractive anymore?" Her defenses dropped and she took his face in her hands, looking at him with surprise and empathy.

"Oh Billy, you are still just as sweet and patient as you were when we were kids. You are *not* wasting your time. If anything, you're even more attractive to me now than ever." She grinned at him and saw the twinkle return to his eyes.

"Then what's up Mag? Do I smell funny or something?" She laughed and knew he was feeling better if he was making one of his jokes during a serious conversation.

"Gawd no!! You smell great!" She was surprised at her prompt answer and blushed a little. He grinned again at her. Then it was her turn to hesitate. Maggie struggled to find the right words. "Billy, I fell for you and lost you once before, and it was one of the hardest things I've ever gone through. I have spent the last 25 years missing you. My husband left me for another woman, taking away any positive ideas I still had left of love and marriage. My heart doesn't want to hurt again, and I just need some time to believe this is for real before letting my walls down." She leaned down and rubbed his nose softly with hers. Then she brushed her lips against his, feeling his chin lift. She kissed him, long and deliberately. He smiled up at her and pulled her close, resting his head on her stomach and hugging her.

"Okay Mag. I'll wait as long as it takes." And she hugged him back.

They exchanged a long goodbye at her door, having a hard time peeling themselves from each other. They kissed and held one another tight, not wanting to let go. As he finally started to leave, he promised to come by the next day for lunch. "Maybe we could try making your famous apple crisp," he jested. She gave him a harmless slap on the arm, and he hugged her closely again and gave her another long kiss.

Maggie watched him walk to her gate before she headed back inside. *That's still one fine ass,* she thought to herself as she watched with a hungry smile. She was so tired from her day, but her heart was so full and floating that she had trouble getting to sleep. She couldn't help but think of what Billy had asked her. She was surprised at his insecurity, then thought about how heated things had gotten and how often she had backed off. Maggie grinned lovingly to herself, hearing his words in her mind, "I'll wait as long as it takes Mag." Her love for him grew stronger every day. She also found herself thinking about the bus again and decided not to fight against the memory. The feeling of straddling Billy again was incredibly enjoyable and tantalizing, and her thoughts wandered even more. She didn't mind the fantasies that were unfolding, and she let them play out in her mind before she finally drifted off.

<h1 style="text-align:center">CHAPTER 11</h1>

When Billy arrived the next day, he had a bag of flour and a bag of cat treats in one hand and a quart of butterscotch ice cream in the other. Maggie heard the door open and went out to meet him in the front hallway, followed closely by Old Bill. "Hey Mag," he said. Then, looking down with a smile, he added, "And Mr. Bill. I came prepared for apple crisp and a happy cat." He grinned as he followed her back into the kitchen. She laughed and went over to the fridge and opened it up.

"Want a cold one with lunch, Billy?" Maggie asked, already reaching in to grab herself a bubbly water.

"Sure Mag, thanks." She grabbed him a beer. Billy walked over to the fridge and popped the ice cream into the freezer. He gave the bag of cat treats a little shake and Bill came running over, watching eagerly as Billy poured a few pieces onto the floor for him. Then they sat at the island and ate the chicken stir fry she had made for them. "Great lunch," he complimented. The two of them gathered up their dishes and took them to the sink. Maggie washed and Billy dried. "So, what else do we need for your famous apple crisp?" he asked.

"Oh, go on Billy!" she responded, thinking he was just teasing her.

"No, really, let's make some crisp together. Teach me the ways of the apple, Mag." She laughed and leaned forward against him playfully.

"Oh, now you are teasing!" Billy washed the apples and then the two of them started peeling. Maggie bent down to find a pan deep in one of the bottom cupboards. Billy took the opportunity to come up behind her to give her butt a little pinch. She stood up quickly, a bit surprised. Then giggling, she turned to give him her best attempt at a stern look. "Now Billy, I thought you wanted to learn the 'way of the apple'? This is no time for goofing around." Billy kissed her forehead and shrugged with a cheeky grin.

Then, standing up straight and saluting her, he said, "Right, terribly sorry Ms. Ashberry." The two of them grinned. They chopped apples together, laughing and flirtatiously bumping into each other as they worked. When they got to the oatmeal and flour, Billy had some all over his hands and leaned over to Maggie, grabbing her face with a cheeky look on his own. Before she could say anything, he pulled her in and kissed her so hard she couldn't even think about complaining. When Billy let go of her face, she raised her hand and let loose the flour she was holding. He laughed through the cloud of flour dust and the two of them giggled at their powdery faces. It took them ages to prepare the crisp, but they had so much fun. By the time it went into the oven, both of them had floury handprints on their butts, powdery hair and faces, and sore bellies from all the laughing they had done. They each washed their hands and then splashed water over their faces in an attempt to get some of the flour off. They headed out back with some fresh cold drinks while they waited for the crisp to bake.

"Now, no dozing off, eh Mag." Billy joked. She threw him a playfully serious look and the two of them laughed again. They chatted about their day apple picking and the many plans for fixing the house together. They had just started laughing at Billy learning how to milk a cow when they heard the oven timer go off.

"Oh Billy, it really is great to spend time with you again. I've really missed you." Maggie said as they went in to dish out the hot, bubbly dessert and add a scoop of ice cream on top.

"Yeah, I'm glad to be here with you too Mag. I'll even stick around if your crisp doesn't turn out. Well, if it's not *too* crisp!" he replied, giving her a little nudge with his arm and grinning at her. "I've really missed you too." He added, his eyes crinkled cheekily as he smiled at her. They sat and enjoyed their dessert together, then enjoyed their usual long goodbye at the door before Billy left for the b and b.

Not long after their baking day, Carla had finally cornered Maggie one day at the bookshop. "Ok Mags, spill the beans! You get'n any yet? You seem perkier than usual!"

Maggie laughed at her friend's eagerness and quickly answered, "No Carla, I'm still not rushing into anything. It's been 25 years for Billy and I - what's a few more months?" Carla's mouth fell open.

"What's a few more months? Mags, are you mental? He's a man. He's got needs. Hell, you do too! And, he's already been waiting for God knows how long, annnd, I heard Skanky 'Puts out Pauline's' been hanging around the bed and breakfast, and she's apparently got her eye on Billy. She heard he's been spending time with you and it's got'er all wound up. She's been waiting around for Billy and then cornering him whenever she gets the chance." Maggie felt her stomach drop but decided to wave off any worry.

"Oh, he wouldn't go for Pauline. Anyway, he's over at my place too often to get the chance." Carla just gave her friend a look.

"You don't know Pauline, Mags!" she argued, but Maggie gave her a face like she didn't want to hear anymore, and Carla dropped the subject.

When Maggie locked up for the day and had started on her way home, she decided to pop into Pat and Stan's to see if Billy was in. Pat saw her come in and motioned to the corner of the restaurant. Maggie peeked around the doorway and saw Billy sitting there with a magazine and coffee. She thanked Pat and went over to his table. He looked up, then realizing it was her standing there, grinned at her. He stood up, gave her a kiss and pulled out the chair across from him.

"Hiya Beautiful, nice surprise!" he said as she sat down.

"Ya, just wanted to ask you something Billy," she said with mischief in her eyes. He looked at her with interest.

"Ask away, ask away."

"Well, are you busy tomorrow morning?"

He thought for a moment, acting like his calendar was so full, then smiled and answered, "No, think I'm free."

"Okay, dress comfortably and pick me up around 8." She stood up, leaned down, and kissed him. Then she flashed him her big smile and said, "See you then Billy." She left him sitting there looking amused and curious.

The next morning, at 8:00 sharp, Maggie heard the bike rumbling out front. She grabbed her coat and headed out to meet him. "Morning Beautiful," he said as she approached. She smiled as she came close enough to give him a kiss and took the helmet he was holding out for her.

"Morning handsome farm boy," she said teasingly, strapping on her helmet and climbing on behind him.

"So, where to?" he asked eagerly.

"The Myers farm please," she answered. Billy turned his head to try and look at her.

"What are you up to Mag?" he asked, sounding a little worried.

"We're not milking anything are we?" Maggie laughed and gave him a squeeze around the middle.

"No Billy, no milking today." He revved up the beast and off they rode. When they pulled into the driveway, they saw Carla walking out of the barn. She waved and started walking towards them with a big grin on her face.

"Hey, you two lovebirds; just finished getting a couple of them saddled up for you Mags." And then she turned around and started walking back the way she came, clearly expecting them to follow her. Billy and Maggie climbed off the bike and Billy threw Maggie a skeptical glance.

"Mag, what have you got planned?" She just smiled at him as they left their helmets on the bike. Maggie took his hand, and they followed Carla. They entered the stable where 2 horses, one Maggie's favourite called Black Beauty, and a spotted brown one named Oatmeal, were saddled and waiting, ready to go.

"Gotta get back to milk'n Mags! You two have fun!" Then Carla laughed at Billy as he stood there with his mouth hanging open. She slapped him on the butt as she passed him and laughed again." Happy ride'n Sweet Cheeks." Billy closed his mouth and looked at Maggie.

"Mag, you could have warned me!" he said, walking over to her.

"Nah, then you might have chickened out," she answered as she looked up at Black Beauty lovingly. "Okay farm boy, ready for your 1st riding lesson?" Maggie gave him a sassy smile, *her* eyes now twinkling.

"Would I get away with saying no?" Maggie shook her head and giggled.

"Okay, take the rope, Billy," she said as she grabbed Black Beauty's lead rope. Billy followed suit and mimicked Maggie as she guided, turned, and walked her horse out of the stable. Once they were out on the driveway, Maggie stopped and turned to Billy. "Ok Billy, we're just going to stick with the circle walk in the front field for now. If we take these two out to the open pastures, they'll want to run, and I wouldn't do that to you," she told him smiling. "Not on your first lesson anyway." Billy looked a little worried.

"Alright Mag," he answered. Just then, Oatmeal gave Billy a little body check with his head. Billy jumped to the side a little and Maggie chuckled.

"Think he likes you," she said to him. She came closer to him and gave him a kiss on the cheek. "Don't worry Billy, he's a gentle guy. Kinda likes to take things slow. I'm sure he'll go easy on you." She winked at him and walked on, Billy following apprehensively. Once they were out in the front field and on the circle path, Maggie closed the gate and tied her lead to the fence. Patting Beauty and running her hand along his side as she walked back to Billy and Oatmeal. "OK, here we go Billy. You alright?" He looked a little pale.

"Ya, sure thing Mag." Maggie reached out and squeezed his hand.

"Just like riding the beast. Well, the original version that is!" He nodded at her trying to smile. She walked back to him, reached her hands up, and wrapped them around his shoulders, standing on her toes and giving him a kiss. "It's gonna be great Billy, you'll see." Weakly, he smiled at her, still looking nervous. She stepped back and said, "First, you need to get up there." She looked up at the horse's back. "So, you put your foot in the stirrup, lift yourself up, and swing the other foot over his back." Maggie gave Oatmeal a pat. Billy looked at her for a moment then gave it a go. He was up in one try but Maggie noticed he was looking a bit nervous. "Great!" she said to him. "Now you can hold the horn," pointing it out on the saddle at the bottom of the horse's neck. "I can take his lead, or you can just hold the reins."

She handed them to Billy. He took them and held on tight, looking a bit awkward astride his horse.

Oatmeal was busily eating the grass at his feet, seemingly unaware of the new rider on his back. Maggie walked over to Beauty, untied him, and climbed on with graceful ease. She turned herself and the horse to face Billy. "Now we'll just go at a gentle trot, to start." Billy nodded, trying once again to smile.

"Mag, this guy won't throw me off, will he?" he asked worriedly.

"No, Oatmeal isn't like that. Not a wild bone in his body. More likely he won't stop eating long enough to even get him walking." They both laughed, looking down at the horse still munching away on the grass.

"Okay, how do I get him going?" Maggie was happy Billy was attempting to be brave. She backed her horse up to stand next to Billy and Oatmeal. Billy looked, with admiration, at how she seemed to have just become part of the horse.

"You look so elegant up there, Mag," he said, smiling at her warmly.

"Thanks," she responded. "I've always felt right at home on a horse," she said with a proud smile. "So, now, all you have to do is make sure you have the reins nice and firm and even. That's how you'll let him know what you want him to do. Pull left, he'll go left; pull right, he'll go right, and if you let them go slack, he'll know he can roam around, okay?" Billy nodded, holding tight. "Now, when you're ready, you give him a light kick or slap him on his rump and say, 'Gee up,' okay?" At Maggie's words, Black Beauty was suddenly eager to get on with it, happily expecting his usual run with Maggie. "Whooooa Beauty," she called as the horse anxiously turned on the spot.

"Okay, now where's the brake?" Billy asked teasingly. They both laughed as he winked at her.

"Just pull back, firmly, on the reins and say whoa." She gave Beauty a little kick, and said, "Easy now." Billy watched the horse back off a little as Maggie walked him up beside Oatmeal again, who was still happily grazing.

"Here goes nothing," Billy said and gave his horse a little kick. Oatmeal just looked up like he wasn't sure when these people had arrived and bent down to eat again. Maggie drew closer and told Billy to hold on, giving Oatmeal a stronger slap on the rump and yelling, "Gee up, Gee up!" Oatmeal started into a slow walk. Maggie grinned as she saw Billy's face break into a smile.

"Looking pretty good up there, Billy," she told him, trotting along beside him.

"Still not too sure about this Mag, but if you can give the beast a go, seems only fair I give horseback riding a go too." Black Beauty whinnied and threw his head back a little. "Is he alright Mag?" Billy asked as Oatmeal sauntered along.

"Yes, he's fine, just wants to go for a run. He's not used to taking it slow." Billy grinned to himself, reaching out and giving Beauty a little pat on the back.

"Know how you feel, Buddy," he said, and Maggie glanced back at him with a bemused look. "We both know she's worth the wait though, don't we?" he added, winking and grinning mischievously as Maggie turned to look at him again. They did one circuit before Oatmeal decided he needed to graze again. Billy laughed and tried to get him going, but Oatmeal kept eating for a few minutes before allowing himself to be encouraged on again. Maggie had them almost at a canter by the time they had finished Billy's lesson. "Thanks, Mag, that was actually really cool," he said as they were on their last lap.

"We should take them out on the trails next time," she suggested. "If you'd like to, that is?"

He grinned at her, "Yes, that would be fun Mag. We could make a day of it." Maggie looked at him and felt warmth course through her. There he was, trying new things with her, happily letting her bend and break his mold a little at a time. And she, slowly, allowed Billy to break her out of the cage she had built around herself, one bar at a time. She had loved young Billy for 25 years now. Of course, that Billy was perfect to her and nothing and no one could ever compare to the blissful week she had based her adoration on. But now, spending time together again, even without sex, she was realizing that he was perfect for her. He *was her* Billy, and her love for him was growing deeper still. She couldn't help but feel like she was dreaming and needed to pinch herself. Moving Beauty as close to Oatmeal as she could, Maggie reached out her hand for Billy's. He took it and she leaned toward him. He leaned closer and they grinned at one another before their lips met. They kissed lovingly until Beauty brayed his complaints at standing idle. They laughed and smiled at one another. Maggie was still lost in her dreamy thoughts of her lifelong love for this gorgeous man next to her.

"Hey, you two!" She was brought back from her thoughts by Carla's voice across the field. Looking up, she saw Carla waving at them. "You kids want some lunch?" she called out. Maggie waved, looking at Billy, and he gave a little shrug and nod.

"Sure Carla," Maggie called back. Beauty was suddenly whinnying anxiously again.

"Hey Mag, why don't you take him for a run? I'll head back to Carla," Billy said. Maggie smiled at him.

"You sure?" she asked, and he nodded with a smile. "Ya, okay, just a quick run, and then I'll join you," she answered happily. Carla was walking towards them now and Billy kept Oatmeal sauntering along until she could take the lead.

"What's Mags up to?" she asked him. But before he could answer, Maggie had given Beauty a kick. They heard the horse whinny loudly. He lifted his front hooves off the ground then landed again. Carla and Billy watched as Beauty started into a swift gallop. Billy couldn't look away. Maggie looked so graceful and free, her hair billowing wildly like waves flowing behind her in the wind. The way she held herself was breathtaking. The confidence that he could see in her as they sped through the field and the happiness on both Maggie's and the horse's faces was tangible.

"She looks even more gorgeous than usual on that animal, doesn't she?" Carla's voice interrupted the moment. Billy came out of his trance slightly, still not taking his eyes off Maggie.

"Yes, she does. Exquisite," he answered, distantly and dreamily. Carla smiled seeing the look on his face. "How does she not fly off, riding that fast?" Billy asked, more to himself than to Carla. Carla laughed.

"Strong legs, Sweet Cheeks. Strong core too." She said as Billy continued staring at Maggie in awe. Maggie and Black Beauty were now headed back. She had a huge grin on her face and Beauty was snorting and whinnying, complaining about having to come back so soon.

"Hey, what are you two gawking at?" Maggie asked Billy and Carla. Carla gave Maggie a secret look behind Billy and tilted her head towards him, mimicking a panting, drooling dog. Maggie laughed out loud, and Billy looked back at Carla, but she quickly went back to just smiling. They walked back towards the stable, Maggie gracefully dismounting before Beauty had even fully stopped. She slid down Beauty's body and landed on the ground like some kind of forest elf.

Then, she walked over to Billy and stood close enough to help him down if he needed her to. He managed pretty well and laughed a little at himself when he landed and started to walk.

"Didn't tell me my ass would go numb, Mag," he said, laughing his deep Billy laugh, Carla and Maggie joining in.

"I could give it a rub for ya Sweet Cheeks!" Carla offered with a hopeful grin. The three of them laughed again. They continued on, to the stable, unbridled the horses, and walked them into their stalls. "Make sure to give Oatmeal a pat and tell him he's a good boy Billy," Carla called out. Billy would have thought she was kidding if he hadn't recently snuggled up with one of her cows. Maggie wiped Beauty down, then loved him up, talking away to him the whole time. The horse nudged its head against Maggie's face and Maggie snuggled him back, giving him another pat before closing the gate. The 3 of them headed into the house and cleaned up for lunch. Stu wasn't home so Carla got some burgers out of the freezer and put Billy in charge of the barbecue. He got it going while Maggie found the toppings and brought them out to the back picnic table.

"So, how'd ya like your ride'n lesson Billy Boy?" Carla asked with a wide smile.

"It was great actually," he answered, sounding a bit surprised.

"Think we're going to go out again," Maggie added. "Maybe do one of the trails."

Carla finished chewing and spoke again. "Oh, that's a good idea you two. Maybe you can find a place for another riding lesson while yer out there!" Maggie threw her a look, and Carla shrugged cheekily. They ate their lunch and chatted away about the farm. Maggie told Billy about when she used to ride in competitions when she was younger.

"Bet you won a lot Mag," he said, smiling. "You ride like you're part of the horse." Maggie laughed at his bemused grin. They helped Carla clean up, thanked her for lunch, and headed back into town.

The next day was spent, once again, mucking around the house with Billy. The two of them caulking windows and hammering in any loose boards or siding that was falling off. They laughed and talked and enjoyed each other's company as usual. Billy took any chance he got to get closer to Maggie, trailing his hand across her arm or waist when she'd come near. Watching her with a captivated stare when he thought she didn't notice. Giving her little kisses here and there if they were close enough while they worked. Maggie reciprocated, but held back quite a bit, trying not to seem too eager or give him the green light but hoping she was still showing enough of her affection for him to keep him interested. Billy mentioned his sore butt and they had a good laugh.

"You get used to it after you do it a few times," was Maggie's advice about his horseback riding experience. She looked over in time to see him rubbing his bottom tenderly.

"Say, that oil rub doesn't work for sore horse-ass does it, Mag?" he asked, grinning at her.

She grinned back, then said, "We'll plan to go again soon. Get you toughened up in no time," and she smiled at him affectionately.

"That would be great Mag, but maybe we should give my ass some time to get over the first ride." The two of them broke out in laughter. They had been working for the better part of the morning when they decided to call it a day and have some lunch. After they had finished eating, Billy stood up and said, "Hey, thanks for lunch Mag, but I need to get going. Got a call about a house just a day or so's ride from here. I thought I'd head out extra early tomorrow and have a look." Maggie felt a strange kind of disappointing worry at his words, but she didn't want him to know that.

"Oh, that's great Billy. It's great you might finally get yourself a house!" And she smiled at him. Billy bent down and gave her a peck on the cheek, smiling back.

"Ya, hope it's worth the drive. See you in a couple of days Mag." And off he went.

Carla's horn beeped early the next morning as she arrived to pick Maggie up for fishing. "Where's Billy?" Carla asked. Maggie told her Billy was gone and wouldn't be back for a couple of days. Carla went quiet, which typically only happened when they were actually fishing.

"What?" Maggie asked, "Why aren't you saying anything?" Carla moved uncomfortably in her seat and opened her mouth to answer, then sat back and closed her mouth again. "Carla!?" Maggie insisted.

"Well, it's probably noth'n Mags, wasn't even going to mention it, but now that you say that… Okay, Mags. Stu was bringing in a load of corn to the grocery store yesterday morning and said he saw Billy and Pauline out front of the bed and breakfast. She was hanging all over'em." Maggie's mouth went dry, and she had to take a drink of her coffee before she spoke again.

"Ya, so, she hangs all over lots of men, what's your point Carla?" Carla stopped and thought for a few seconds before answering.

"Well, Mags, it's just that he also mentioned her hopping on his bike with him just as Stu was walking in with the corn." Maggie's heart sank but she tried to act like it was nothing.

"Well, I'm sure it's nothing." she answered. But she couldn't shake the feeling that maybe she had waited too long with Billy. Maybe he was just like so many men, and had no problem messing around. That, as Carla put it, "He's a man, he had needs, and he'd already waited for

God knows how long," was only too true, and maybe, Maggie thought to herself, he took Pauline for more than just a bike ride. Their fishing day was even quieter than usual. On the way home, Carla tried to cheer her up, and Maggie tried her best to fake indifference.

It had been a couple days since Billy left. Maggie was certain she'd lost him to the town tramp for sure. *Oh Maggie, you really blew it now!* was all she could think. She hadn't gone into the shop since fishing with Carla. She was too down to face anyone. Carla had stopped by to see Maggie on the second night of her "hermitting" to check she was doing alright.

"Where've you been Mags?! Haven't seen you for days!" she asked when she came in for a quick visit. "Geeze Mags, looking awful scruffy aren't ya?" Maggie didn't answer. She just grabbed a couple of bubbly waters for the two of them and plunked herself down on a stool at the kitchen island. "Hey Mags, I saw 'Puts Out Pauline' on my way over." Maggie looked up at her friend.

"Yeah, so, what do I care?" was her response.

"Well, it's just that I wondered if Billy was back yet?" Carla looked genuinely concerned and reached a hand out to give Maggie's arm a squeeze. Maggie gave her a forced grin, shaking her head.

"Nah, I haven't seen him since the other day when he left." Then she got up and grabbed a Kleenex and gave her nose a good snort.

"Well, maybe she didn't go with him then Mags," Carla pressed. Maggie shrugged again. "So, what've you been up to then?" Carla looked around the kitchen and living room before going on. "You've just been sitting around in your pjs, eating cheesecake, watching sad, old, black-and-white romance movies, and snuggling Old Bill, haven't ya?" Her friend definitely knew her well.

"Ya, maybe, something like that. Say Carla, I think I'm going to take a nap. Thanks for popping in though." Maggie ushered Carla out the door.

She just caught Carla saying, "You should shake yourself outta your stupor Mags! Get yourself cleaned up at least," as she closed the door and locked it behind her.

Maggie spent the next day, still in her pjs, moping around the house again. She'd run out of cheesecake and had moved on to finishing the rest of the ice cream that Billy had brought for the apple crisp. She was reminiscing, feeling bluer and bluer, when she remembered there was an old box up in the attic somewhere. She knew that it was full of keepsakes and such. So up she went, and after searching through a number of boxes and moving a few things around, she found it. She opened it up and peeked inside, seeing a fuzzy blue sweater on top of a few loose pictures. She knew it was the box she was looking for. Down she climbed, carefully carrying the box. She walked downstairs and sat it on the floor next to the couch. Maggie picked up the sweater, absentmindedly bringing it to her face and smelling it. She thought she could still smell Billy after all these years. Then she smiled sadly to herself, feeling like it was just her mind tricking her. Putting the sweater aside, she pulled out some old photo albums and was deep down memory lane, with Bill curled up beside her on the couch.

Maggie sat, smiling at the photos of her and her family when she was still just a little girl. Her first time milking a cow and riding Benny, her first horse. There was even a funny one of her when she was only about 4, covered in muck from the pigpen. She had spent the morning rolling around with them, happy as could be. There were random ones of her and her brothers playing in the yard. A couple photos of her on her horse, winning ribbons at competitions. Her nurses' graduation photo, in her uniform and a big smile on her face. Family picnics mostly with her mom, as her dad had spent most of his time running the farm. She smiled softly, thinking of her parents and missing them. She sat remembering how hard the two of them had worked and what a strong team they had been. Maggie turned to the next page of the album and was now facing her teen years. She realized most of these pictures were still pictures of her working on the farm. *Wow,* she thought, *I really did spend a lot of energy and time working on that farm.*

A few pictures of her teen years with old friends that she'd lost touch with years ago. She chuckled to herself at their brightly coloured outfits and big hairdos. Remembering the days when she was more carefree, before she had so many responsibilities, and began losing herself. She now picked up a little green book and smiled when she opened it. It had pictures of her week at the cabin in it. Maggie and her friends grinning and goofing around for a few group photos. There were some of the other group mixed in with her group too; there was even one with everybody who had stayed that week, except Tina who had taken the picture. She and Billy were sitting on the floor at the front. Billy was behind her with his arms draped over the front of her shoulders and Maggie was holding his hands. Maggie laughed out loud at some silly pictures of the group clowns showing off in the background or pulling faces for the camera. Pictures of skiing and building snowmen. Snowball fights and nights at the fire pit. Some faces were clear in the light of the fire, and others she couldn't figure out anymore. One, she knew, was Billy because of the guitar in his lap, although you couldn't really see his face. She even found a couple of them skinny dipping, too dark to really see anything clearly. Then she found some pictures she had totally forgotten about. Some great pictures of them all dressed up in their fancy clothes, Becky and Justin in their matching onesies, a few people break dancing, Maggie, Bridget, and Tina in pretty dresses, grinning broadly.

Stuck in the back of the album, under another photo, was a picture of her and Billy. They couldn't have been closer if they were one person. Arms and legs wrapped tightly around each other, a big smile on Maggie's face and Billy giving her a big kiss on the cheek. It looked like they were on the common room couch. She suddenly remembered that someone had grabbed her camera and snuck up to get a picture of the two of them rolling about together in one of their many make out sessions! *No wonder it was hidden*, she thought to herself. "I can't believe I forgot about these," she said out loud, staring at her and Billy, so young and happy. She sat there for ages, just looking at the two of them wrapped up together. She couldn't help but smile. Then she felt a wave of sadness again. Self-doubt and critical self-talk began rearing their ugly heads. Just then the phone rang. She jumped out of her thoughts. It rang again, but she just sat there. What if it was him? She wasn't ready to talk to him yet. Maggie listened as it rang a few more times before the machine picked up.

"Hey Mags," came Carla's voice. "You there? Mags? Just check'n you're still live'n. Okay, well, call me when you get this." Then, she heard Carla hang up, and the machine cut off. She put the pictures back into the box and closed it up again, making her way slowly to the kitchen to feed Old Bill. She grabbed another bubbly water for herself. Then, it was back to the couch, where she pulled Billy's old sweater on and flopped down. That's where she spent the rest of the day, lost in thought, and watching whatever she could find on the TV.

On the fourth day, Maggie decided enough was enough. Carla was right. She needed to shake herself out of this stupor and get on with it. She got herself showered and dressed and decided to clean up the mess she'd made in her depressed state. As always, music was the only real way to cheer her up and get herself motivated when she just felt like being blue and lazing about. She couldn't resist dancing to a good song and singing along, so she cranked the radio and got to tidying up. She finished vacuuming the living room and threw out the empty cheesecake boxes and the many Kleenexes lying around. Then, she started to make a dent in the kitchen, still dancing and singing her heart out.

CHAPTER 12

Maggie was at the kitchen sink, still washing up, singing and sexily dancing to one of her favourite songs called "Cry to Me" when suddenly, Billy was right behind her.

He held her hips, pressing himself up close with his lips resting on her neck as he softly spoke, "I missed you, Mag." Then he joined in the dance with her. At first, she felt like turning around and punching him in the gut, but as he moved against her to the music and she felt his breath on her neck, she lost all ability to think. She could only feel overwhelming angst within and felt her pulse start to quicken rapidly. The surprise and the unexpected contact were quite arousing. She almost came right then and there! The suddenness of his body, warm and nestled up against the back of hers. His lips were slightly wet and hot on her neck, nuzzling into her hair and breathing deeply near her ear. "Mmm, you always smell so good Maggie." He breathed. His hands ran down her thighs and back up to her hips as they seductively moved to the sensual sway of the song. She had put the dishes in her hands down to reach around behind her and grab onto his hips, moving the two of them even closer together.

His hands were everywhere now, just slightly skipping the more personal areas, but close enough to make her ache. They wandered across her stomach, down her hips, over her neck and chest. She had reached her hands up to the back of his neck now, running her fingers through his hair. He started kissing her neck and her breathing quickened. They were grinding so deeply that they were practically one. He moved his face straight behind her head, lifting her long hair and kissing up the nape of her neck. She could hardly breathe. Billy was breathing heavily. Their bodies pushed harder against one another. The song played on and still, they kept moving against each other. Into each other, and with each other, in time to the music. Her hands came back down to his hips, and she reached for his "sweet cheeks".

He was back to kissing the side of her neck and she pressed herself into him, deeply and erotically swaying her hips. And then, the song was over, and he spun her around. She could hardly stand up. Letting her head fall back and dropping into his hands as he leaned down and kissed her with such intensity that she felt like she was flying. He softly kissed down her neck, to the top of her chest, still holding her head in his hands. He kissed his way back up and found her lips again. The kiss lasted ages and she thought she might melt on the spot. When she felt the swaying starting up again, she reached up and clasped his wrists as he held her head, and she looked up into his face. The powerful anticipation in his expression made her almost give in to temptation. She truly wanted him at that moment, but her heart was still telling her no.

"I missed you too, Billy," she said, already starting into her gentle sendoff routine. But before she could go on, he stepped back, holding her hands in his.

With an almost bewitched look on his face, Billy said, "Your effing hot Mag." They both gave a little, shuddery laugh. He grabbed her, pulled her towards him, and kissed her again. She put her hands up on his chest, gently pushing him away.

"I think you better go Billy." He gave her another kiss.

"You sure about that Mag?" he asked. She nodded and took a small step backward, feeling like she was drugged with raging hormones. He pulled her in closer, giving her another kiss. "Really sure Mag?" he asked. His eyes were so deep and dark she could hardly stand the magnetic pull between them. She nodded again, ever so slightly, unable to speak. Billy gave her one last kiss before making his way out of the kitchen, stopping once more to look back at her, almost pleadingly. Maggie wanted him to stay, so badly but still felt she couldn't take the plunge. She smiled at him, one hand sliding up her body and resting on her heaving chest, the other reaching up and touching her bottom lip, then sliding down to meet the other on her chest.

"See ya Billy," she managed to say.

He winked at her, and before he turned around and walked out of the kitchen he said, "Wouldn't fancy another swim in the lake would you Mag? It's just that I think it might be a good idea if I went for a cold dip." She laughed a little, thinking it was probably best not to mention the cold water had the opposite effect on her. Seductively smiling at him, her green eyes deep and warm, she shook her head slightly. Their eyes locked and they smiled at each other. Then Billy turned and walked out of the kitchen. Maggie heard the front door open and as he left, she heard him say to himself, "Damn."

Carla popped into the bookshop the next day with a big grin on her face. "Glad to see you outta your pjs and back to work, Mags!" Maggie smiled at her.

"Morning Carla. Yeah, a good friend shook me out of it." Carla smiled back at her.

"Just wondering if you want to come out to the farm later? Stu got'emself a new grill and wants to have somebody over so he can show'r off." Maggie laughed.

"Ya, for sure Carla, sounds good." Carla smiled happily. "Thought you might need an evening out with friends, get your mind off pining for Billy." Maggie grinned whimsically back at Carla.

"Billy's back Carla. Stopped by last night." Carla's mouth fell open.

"Ya and did you let'm have it Mags?" Carla jumped on the spot, with her fists up in the air. Maggie laughed at her friend and answered, smiling.

"No. But I think we're gonna be okay." Now Carla just looked a bit confused.

"What do you mean, Mags? What's that look about you?" she asked, pointing at Maggie and tracing her finger in the air at her. "You guys didn't 'make up' did ya?" Maggie couldn't help but grin.

"Oh Mags, you didn't? You finally cleared the cobwebs, didn't ya!?" Maggie laughed again.

"No, not an official clearing, but we did some, um, dusting." Maggie turned around quickly and busied herself needlessly with a few books that looked like they could use repiling. More so because she couldn't stop grinning and didn't want to look Carla in the eye anymore.

"Oh, come on, you gotta tell me more! Ah, shit, tell me now! Quick Mags." Maggie shook her head with a giggle. "Well, if Billy's back, bring him too of course. Gotta run. Oh shit, can't wait to hear about this," she said anxiously. Maggie heard the door open and turned back around, laughing at her friend's desperation.

"Okay, Carla. See you later, and I'll see if Billy's interested."

Carla stopped and looked back behind her with a smirk, "Oh, I'd say he's mighty interested, Mags." Then, before Maggie could respond, she was out the door.

"Sure, it sounds like a laugh, Mag. What time should I pick you up?" was Billy's response when he popped in that afternoon. She flashed him a big smile.

"I don't know. Sevenish, I suppose." Maggie had made sandwiches for them today for lunch. Nothing fancy, just some leftover roast and mayo. "So, we didn't really get a chance to talk last night. What did you think of that house you went to see Billy?" she asked as they ate. She was hoping to find out whether he'd been alone or not. She was also hoping that he didn't like the house and that things would stay just the way they were without Billy moving out of town.

"Not really what I was looking for, Mag. Guess it wasn't the right fit," was his response, as he looked straight into her eyes, his deep stare lingering for a moment. They weren't as chatty as usual today, and he headed out shortly after lunch, saying he'd be back to pick her up later. Maggie hoped she hadn't blown it with him. She also hoped nothing had happened with Pauline. She wanted to know but didn't want to ask him. Just the thought of the two of them together made her skin crawl. She wasn't even sure if she could touch him again if something had happened between them. She decided to have a shower and maybe even shave her legs. *Cause, you never know,* she thought to herself. She laughed at how much she was feeling like a silly, love-struck teen again. She put on her best fitting, ass-pleasing jeans and a black, thin, strapped tank top with a little peach-coloured sweater over top. She left her hair down. Now that the summer humidity was gone, her curls were less frizzy and behaving themselves nicely.

She sat down at her vanity, grabbed her vanilla oil, and rolled it over her neck and shoulders, then on her wrists, rubbing them together. She added a drop of lavender to her hands, rubbed them together, then scrunched her fingers into her curls. Maggie reached up for her black velvet choker with the little teardrop pearl in the center and did it up around her neck. Her mind was now drifting to the night Billy gave her his necklace. She reached over and pulled out a little drawer in her jewelry box, hoping to find it. There were a couple of old rings that were too small but she'd kept for sentimental reasons, and a bracelet her youngest brother had made her on her eighteenth birthday. There was also a charm bracelet that belonged to her Mom, which she picked up and admired with fond memories. The charms always fascinated her as a child. She thought it was so neat to have a piece of jewelry that told your story. Her mom's had a little gold Bible, a silver horse, a green four-leaf clover, a double heart with a gold ring around it, a 16, and a 25. There were also some pretty, gem-like stone beads in different colours and a little tarnished key. She put the bracelet down, smiling, and looked into the bottom of the little drawer. The gold chain *was* still there. She was tempted to put it on instead of her choker, but she hadn't worn it in years and thought Billy probably wouldn't even recognize it anyway. Lots of people had gold chains, and she looked up at herself in the mirror and thought the choker looked nice with her outfit. As she sat there looking at herself, she went from feeling like a silly young girl to recognizing what a beautiful woman she had become.

Being on her own had helped her grow so much and this newfound confidence that was growing inside her was allowing her to appreciate herself more than she had in decades. Maggie heard Billy pull up on his bike and went downstairs. She grabbed her leather jacket and the 6 pack she'd picked up to take to Carla and Stu's. Then, she closed the front door and almost ran down the stone path to meet Billy.

"Wow Mag, you look amazing," he said as he handed her a helmet. She smiled at him, sticking the 6 pack on the back of the bike, and then climbed on behind him.

"You're looking pretty fine yourself," she replied, wrapping her arms around him, and giving him a squeeze. "Mmm, you smell so good," she said as she snuggled up to him.

"You know, we could get lost on our way to Carla and Stu's farm. Maybe find a cozy spot under a tree, spend the night under the moonlight." She laughed a little and gave him another squeeze.

"Sounds nice Billy, but Carla would be out with the dogs looking for me." Billy fired up the engine; the radio was playing "Silver Lining" as they pulled out of the driveway and headed for the Myer's farm for the evening.

When they arrived at the little farm, they could hear Carla and Stu out back. It sounded as if they were having a fight. "Oh great, looks like we've already missed the fun part," Maggie joked as they walked around back. Billy took her hand in his and pulled her back. She spun on the spot, twirling in towards him and landing up against him. He bent down and planted a big kiss on her mouth. His hands slid into her back jean's pockets, giving her butt a firm squeeze. She felt giddy, and after a little grin at each other, they started for the backyard again. Before they reached the corner of the house, Maggie pulled Billy back, sat the 6 pack down, then stood back up and pushed Billy up against the house. He looked a little surprised and before he could comment, while still holding him against the wall, Maggie tugged on his jacket. She pulled him down enough so that she could kiss him, pressing herself firmly against him as she slipped him the tongue. She grabbed his face, kissing him more intensely, and their tongues swirled around each other, stirring up heated exhilaration within both of them.

As she released him from her grip and their lips unlocked, she looked up to see an enchanted sort of dazed look on Billy's face. She grinned at him and squeezed his butt. Then, she picked the 6 pack back up. Taking his hand, they proceeded around the corner of the house where Carla and Stu were standing at the grill. The two of them suddenly went quiet, and Carla was all smiles. She came over to hug Maggie and welcomed them both.

"Drink?" she asked them, and they followed her over to Stu and said hello.

"Glad you're alright and back to your old self." Billy said, hanging back with Stu. Billy still had a funny expression on his face as Carla and Maggie went in to grab some cold ones and put Maggie's 6 pack in the fridge.

"What was that about Carla?" Maggie asked while they were still in the kitchen. Carla stopped and turned to Maggie.

"Oh just effing Stu going on about Billy and 'Puts Out Pauline'! Told'em to keep his mouth shut tonight. That we didn't even know if anything went on." Maggie felt a little sick at the thought but decided to let it go and enjoy her night. Stu cooked up some big steaks and baked potatoes, and the four of them shared some laughs, enjoying their meal together. Billy seemed to be taking any chance he had to touch Maggie, even if was just running a hand along her shoulder or waist as she walked past him. Maggie found herself doing the same without holding back as much. She even snuck in an unexpected slap when Billy bent over to stoke the fire. He looked back, surprised, but his eyes were twinkling, and she felt herself blushing. Once the sun started to set, Stu got the fire roaring in the pit and turned the radio on in the old pick-up, his favourite country station cranked right up. It didn't take Billy long to coax Maggie up for a dance. Like two youngsters, they danced the night away. Weaving together like a well-seasoned couple, singing along to "Fish'n In The Dark," so comfortable and lighthearted together. Billy swung Maggie around, dipping her at the end of "Keep Me Rocking," having fun dancing to "Boot Scoot'n Boogie" and "That Summer." Maggie would fall back into his arms, the two of them hugging and getting in a few kisses every once and a while. At one point, Carla dragged Maggie into the kitchen again, telling the guys they were just grabbing a few more beers. Really, she just wanted to ask Maggie about how things were going.

"Shit Mags, you guys look like a couple of randy teens!" Maggie couldn't stop smiling. She felt like she was back at the cabin all over again.

"Oh Carla, I think I'm falling hard again," she answered with a goofy grin that she couldn't seem to wipe off her face.

"No doubt about it, you've got it bad girl." Maggie filled Carla in on their heated dance in her kitchen. "Whoa Mags, that's pretty steamy!" was Carla's response. The two of them giggled like schoolgirls and then went back out to join the guys. They were still enjoying the night together until, without any notice, Stu had reached his "nice" limit of pickled, and he started up again about Pauline. He had made his way over to Billy who was standing by the fire.

"So, see ya been getting your kicks anywhere you can eh, bud?" giving Billy a hardy nudge.

"What's that?" asked Billy, trying to laugh Stu off.

"Seen ya enjoying 'ol'well used Pauline' the other day before the two of ya disappeared on your hog." Stu was starting to waver on the spot and Maggie gave Carla a look, but Carla was already out of her chair and hopping in front of Stu, right up in his face.

"Listen, Stu, you better shut your cake hole quick." Stu laughed, trying to move her aside.

"Ah, just having some fun Carla, like Billy here. Guess you might as well get it as often as you can, eh Billy?" He moved a little closer to

Billy, almost losing his balance as he walked.

"Now that's enough Stu! Stop being such an arse-hole!" yelled Carla, but Maggie and Billy were already headed in the opposite direction.

"Thanks for dinner guys," Maggie called back.

"Sorry Mags," Carla called out, but Maggie and Billy were already around the side of the house headed for the bike.

"Wow, that guy sure knows how to have a good time, eh?" Billy joked. Maggie didn't say anything. She climbed on behind Billy, and they headed back to her house. When they got there, Billy turned off the bike ready to climb off. Maggie quickly stopped him and spoke.

"Thanks, Billy," and she handed him the helmet. "Think I'll just head into bed." He looked surprised and disappointed and seemed to be at a loss for words. As Maggie turned to walk away, he grabbed her arm and stopped her, now getting off the bike as well.

"Mag, you, okay?" he asked, trying to pull her in. She didn't respond. "Mag? Is this about Stu's comment? Nothing happened with Pauline. I didn't even take her for a ride. She climbed on but I asked her to get off. Mag, please, you don't really think I'd be interested in her, do you?" Maggie didn't want to have this conversation. She couldn't even let herself think for a moment that someone like that had touched him, or that he had possibly touched her back. And she certainly didn't want to have such a serious conversation with someone she wasn't sure was even going to stick around.

"Billy, it's none of my business what you get up to. You don't have to explain yourself to me." She spoke calmly and quietly as she felt the tears welling up in her eyes, but she managed to hold them in. She didn't want him to know just how much she had fallen for him again. He was still holding her arm and tried to pull her close, but she resisted.

"Don't worry about it. I'll see you around, okay Billy?" With a look of desperation, Billy let her go. It was a while before she heard him pull away. She kept fighting the urge to run back out and stop him.

Maggie saw Carla the next day. She kept apologizing for Stu's behavior, but Maggie waved it off, knowing it had been the many whiskeys that had followed the many beers talking. Having Stu say what her heart had been dreading really had been too much, though. She wanted to believe Billy but hadn't seen many examples of loyal men in her life. Why would he be any different? Her doubtful self-talk seemed to be winning the conversation currently going on in her mind. What did they really know about each other? She had a week-long fling 25 years ago and now allowed herself to trust and fall for, basically, a stranger. It just wasn't meant to be.

"Saw Billy when I was dropping off the bed and breakfast mail yesterday morning. Not looking so good Mags," said Carla. Maggie didn't respond. She was sure she wasn't looking so good herself, right now. "Are you going to call him?" Carla asked cautiously.

"Why Carla? So you don't have to keep worrying about me?!" Maggie realized immediately that she had responded harshly. "Sorry Carla, guess it's bothering me more than I'm admitting to myself." Carla waved it off.

"No sweat Mags. Love's an awful tricky business."

CHAPTER 13

Maggie didn't talk to Billy for a few days and decided to try not to think about him. He had left messages, but she hadn't responded to him. Telling herself she was fine without him, and that Stu's accusations hadn't mattered to her. It wasn't really working but she faked it as best she could. All she kept thinking was how stupid she felt for giving in and letting her guard down. She hated herself for admitting that she loved him.

"You know Mags," Carla said one day when the two of them were at The Mugs and Saucers for coffee. "He's hurt'n for ya!" Maggie looked up from sipping her coffee, trying to act like she didn't know what her friend meant.

"What are you on about Carla - hurting how?" Carla laughed gruffly.

"Oh, come on Mags, poor guy's probably bluer than a blue-footed booby." Maggie choked on her mouthful of coffee, laughing involuntarily.

"God Carla, that's kinda rude!" Carla took a big gulp of her coffee and swallowed her mouthful of scone.

"Oh, get off it Mags, you two were all over each other at the farm. And that dirty dancing the two a ya were up to! Gawd, and the way he looks at you almost makes *me* weak in the knees," she said, winking at her. "If you had'em they'd be blue by now too!" The two of them cackled the afternoon away, which was exactly what Maggie needed. A good laugh was great medicine. Unfortunately, the effects of the laughter didn't last as long as she would have liked and all Maggie could think was, *You don't know the half of it Carla.*

Carla managed to get a couple more hits in, trying to coax Maggie into calling him and finally letting her hair down, "all the way" before she finished her coffee and headed home. Maggie laughed to herself, feeling her cheeks flush a bit at the thought. It had been so long since she'd been completely intimate with a man. Longer than she cared to calculate. Yes, there had been a few kisses here and there, and always a hug hello and goodbye. There had been those make out sessions with Billy since he came back into her life, and she admitted there had been times it felt like they were a couple. There had even been those few times when things had gotten hot and heavy, but she really couldn't imagine being naked with anyone again. *Well,* she thought to herself, *not out of the lake naked.* Especially, not after he had seen her in her prime. Twenty-five years causes a lot of changes to a body. She grinned to herself as she started down the main street and headed for home.

As she passed the bed and breakfast, the door opened. Her heart skipped, anticipating seeing Billy. Instead, when she looked up, it was to see Pauline wrapped around one of the local farm boys, locked in a sloppy-looking kiss. The guy she was with didn't look old enough to be married, which according to Carla was out of character for the usual husband snatcher. Pauline stepped out and saw Maggie standing there.

"Oh, hey there honey. 'Spose you'd like a picture eh, see'n as your man's a bit of a dud. Doesn't seem very interested in having any fun, does he?" Maggie stepped aside to let her pass.

"Sorry?" Maggie questioned.

"Wasted a lot of my precious time on that Billy boy, think'n he might not fancy the ladies after all," answered Pauline. She clicked her tongue with disgust and flipped her hair as she turned away. "Well, maybe you can bring'em back darling. He doesn't seem to know a good thing when he sees it anyways, even when it's handed to him on a silver platter." Pauline laughed mockingly at Maggie and winked at the young farm boy before he shut the door. And then Pauline strutted the other way up the street. Maggie stood there for a moment, not really sure what she was feeling. *What a piece of work*, she thought to herself. "Silver platter?" She shook her head. Well, sounds like Billy was telling the truth if "Puts Out Pauline's" got her nose out of joint and is on to her next dish.

Still shaking her head, she walked home and was lost in deep thought as she reached the gate and crossed her garden. As she climbed the porch stairs, she saw a small box sitting in front of her door. She picked it up and took it inside with her. Written across the top were the words "Happy Birthday Mag." Nothing else indicated where it came from. It was just an ordinary brown box that had tape wrapped over the top keeping it closed. She took it inside to the kitchen island and sat it down. The box was light and whatever was in it moved around loosely in the box. Maggie sat down on a stool, pulled the tape off the top, opened the flaps, and looked inside. Her heart almost dropped into her stomach.

"No!" She whispered out loud. "He can't have," and she reached in and pulled out her old silver locket. She held it in her hand, staring at it in disbelief. Holding it to her chest and closing her eyes with a grin. Then, opening her hand and looking down at it again, she noticed something was sticking out from the edges of the heart. She opened it up to find a picture of herself on one side and a picture of Billy on the other side. She looked at it for a moment, smiling tenderly. It was a much younger Maggie and Billy. She smiled again, feeling all the years of love for Billy fill her up. Maggie did it up around her neck. She held it close to her heart for a moment, still smiling to herself. *Wow, Billy. Maybe you are the real deal.*

She looked up at the clock, noticed it was approaching half past four and decided to get herself something to eat. She stood up, still smiling to herself, holding the locket to her chest, and walked around the island into the kitchen. She decided to whip up some scrambled eggs and toast. She fed Old Bill his dinner and then headed out back to eat hers. She was thinking about calling Billy and letting him know she believed him, to apologize and thank him for the locket. Maggie picked up the phone and dialed his number. She let it ring a few times, then hung up quickly, deciding she'd call him later. Maybe she would ask him if he wanted to meet for breakfast. She finished the last of her dinner and sat enjoying the lovely evening. Lost in thought again, dreaming of their bodies wrapped together, she could almost feel his energy embracing her. She was feeling a bit amorous and frisky thinking about him and seemed to have some extra energy after her coffee chat with Carla. So seeing as old habits die hard, she set herself to work to keep her thoughts and desires at bay. She was working away on the ivy in the back garden, listening to her oldies station on the radio, when she heard the back gate swing open.

"Hey, I've been worried about you. Thought maybe you'd left the country when you didn't return my calls." Billy said with a chuckle. "What are you up to Mag?" He asked, grinning at her. She never tired of that voice. *Oh, how I've missed the way he says my name*, she thought with a quiver. That deep, husky voice still sent electricity up her spine after all these years. She looked down from the step ladder and smiled at him.

"Just hanging the ivy back up," she answered, turning back to the job at hand. She could feel him looking at her and felt his insatiable energy as he drew closer. She knew she couldn't stay angry with him.

"You haven't changed a bit, Mag! Up on a ladder in a dress and rubber boots." Maggie turned in time to see that sexy grin and those smiling eyes looking up at her. An old, familiar warmth washed over Maggie. There had always been such a strong pull between them. It was palpable in their youth, and now as their eyes met, she was pleasantly surprised to feel it still. It was just as strong between them. Yet, she felt a new level of depth in the energy between them, rising with such a force. Strong and fierce and yet with a softness she thought must come from such a long history between two souls. *I guess it wasn't just the urgent lust of youth*, she thought to herself as she felt his hand on her leg. It moved from her knee to the back of her thigh, the soft material of her skirt moving with his hand as he caressed her leg. Sparks, electric and bursting from inside of her! It had been so long since she last felt such a stirring within. These past weeks together had revived such intense desires in Maggie. He reached up his hand to help her climb down the ladder, facing him. As Maggie reached the last step, Billy stopped her, arms on either side of the ladder causing her to sit down on the nearest step as he pressed himself against her. He looked down at the locket and smiled, then peered deeply into her eyes. It was as if she could see the whole universe between them.

"Thanks for taking care of my heart, Billy," she said to him, reaching out and brushing his cheek softly. He smiled at her again with such longing, hunger, and desire in his dark blue eyes. She felt a shift in who was holding the power now. A surrender was happening inside her and she no longer wanted to cage the passion waiting urgently within. He brushed back the curls around her left ear, smiled, and reached up his other hand to cradle her head in his hands, combing his thick, strong fingers through her hair as he held her.

"I'm sorry Mag. I never intended to hurt you," he said, inches away from her face. She smiled and reached up her hands to hold his face.

"I know Billy. Just a stupid misunderstanding. I'm sorry too." Then, he leaned in closer, and with a warmth like no other, his lips met hers. Maggie knew they were past the "just reconnecting catch up between old friends" kisses. She was done keeping him at bay. She wanted him and he wanted her. The prison walls that she had built around herself had finally come down. They embraced like they would fall apart if they didn't hold onto each other tighter and tighter. Wrapping her legs around his hips, she pulled him as close to her as she could. His hot breath was now on her cheek, then passing her ear.

"Oh Mag," he breathed. Now he was kissing her neck, softly, slowly, lingering. She felt his nose sliding up her neck and back to her ear. His breath sent shivers through her body. Her arms and hands held him tightly and he scooped her up from the ladder. Her legs were wrapped around his waist, her arms around his shoulders. He carried her into the house. "It's always been you Mag," he said, as he carried her. She could feel every breath rising and falling with his chest against her breasts, pressed so tightly against him. As he carried her in, Maggie felt the years melting away. No time had passed for them at this moment, just life lessons, experience, and deeper roots between them. Even after so many years and so much distance between them and not knowing exactly what they really wanted, the universe led them back to each other, over miles and time. He kissed her neck again, so tenderly. His lips were so hot and soft on her skin. Maggie was now pulling up his shirt so she could slide her hands up to caress his strong, still muscular, back. She felt the muscles moving under her fingers as he held her up, his hands under her dress now, running up her legs and squeezing her bottom.

She ran her nails gently up his spine and he suddenly turned the two of them, pinning her against the wall near the staircase, pushing himself harder against her. She ripped open the top buttons of his shirt and pulled it over his head, nibbling on his ear lobe and gently trailing her fingers over the hair on his broad chest. Billy inhaled sharply and pushed her up against the wall again. She could now feel just how strong and thick he still was as she reached down and undid his belt and jeans, running her hand down the front inside of his pants and grasping him in her hand. She felt his hips push forward and heard him inhale deeply. As he held her up with his body, he undid the top of her dress and she lifted her chin in pure anticipation as he kissed down her neck. Then, he found his way to the top of her breasts, reaching up with one hand, cupping and massaging. They suddenly became animals, full of wild passion, licking and sucking and biting and kissing with such a hunger, neither of them able to stand it much longer. She needed to feel release, and only he held the key.

"Oh my God, I want you so bad," she found herself saying out loud. Now his hands were ripping off her underwear as she released him from his own. Clawing at his back, as he grabbed her breasts. Sucking on his neck, pinching, and pulling at her nipples, squeezing his ass, and then "Oh God Billy, " he was inside her. Billy pushed their bodies against the wall, writhing in ecstatic exhilaration, rhythmically rocking their bodies together. The years of longing for each other escalated to a climax. The weeks of tantalizing anticipation were now unleashed with such frenzied passion. Sliding in and out of Maggie, hard and fast and so deep. Then he slid her slowly down the wall, over to the chaise lounge, still inside of her, just a little, almost all the way out, taunting her with the tip of himself. Then, as he laid her down, Billy was sliding slowly and fully all the way back in, almost growling with pleasure together. His lips kissing and sucking her breasts, his tongue circling her nipples. Maggie felt her body rising and falling, watching as her chest lifted with pleasure, running her nails up and down his back and squeezing his ass. Pulling him in deeper.

They were both moaning and moving together. "Ohh, Maggie, you feel so good." Cumming now, kissing each other harder, she held him tight inside of her.

"Billy!" Maggie called out, now feeling his held breath bursting out with a sudden pelvic thrust as he "Aww", exploded inside of her, now softly falling together; still caressing, falling, kissing, and rocking slower and slower, their bodies still gliding in rhythm with each other. Their mingling sweat was hot and wet as their bodies slowed completely. With hearts racing, and chests heaving, they fell, embraced in each other's arms.

They lay there naked, skin to skin, Maggie's face pressed against Billy's chest, his breathing still strong and fast. As she started to gently kiss his chest, she found her way up to his lips. Maggie pressed her lips hard against his, breathing each other in; not kissing, just pressing their lips together and moving slowly against one another. As she felt him leave her body, she gave his bottom lip a playful bite. He kissed her again, holding her head with one hand and caressing her body with the other. They just kept inhaling deeply, pressed so tightly together, until they drifted off to sleep in each other's arms.

CHAPTER 14

They awoke to the sun shining in the front window on their faces. They were impressed at their ability to still go at it like animals but felt the pains of two people who had passed out on a narrow chaise lounge. This made them laugh at their attempt at recreating their youth.

"Well," he chuckled playfully. "That was… wow." Maggie hugged him and smiled.

"Yes, it was, 'wow'. I didn't know it could still be so intense, you know, after all these years." Billy sat up next to her and wrapped his arms around her, pulling her close. He kissed her forehead softly.

"You know Mag, I think we ought to try that again sometime. Maybe next time we'll make it upstairs?" he said, winking at her.

"Is that an invitation?" she asked flirtatiously.

"More like a promise," he answered, standing up and pulling her towards him.

"I really didn't think I'd ever do that again Billy. I was quite sure those days were long gone." Billy squeezed her close and kissed her lovingly. "I'm glad life has brought us back together," she added. Then Maggie stood up on her tiptoes and held his head, gently pulling him down towards her and kissing him. He embraced her, kissing her back, and she felt her whole body soften. She felt so safe and loved in his arms.

"Guess I'll be sticking around, eh Mag? Better extend my payment plan at Pat and Stan's." He smiled his cheeky smile at her.

"No, I don't think you better do that Billy," was Maggie's response. She saw a look of disappointed confusion on his face. "I think it might be better if you moved your stuff in here with me," she added. Billy grinned at her.

"You know, so you can help me finish the house of course." He grabbed her and picked her up off the floor, laughing and spinning them on the spot. As he let her slide back down, she wrapped her arms around his middle, hugging him completely. His strong arms wrapped around her body tightly. And there they stood, finally and fully holding on, knowing they'd never have to let go again.

THE END

About the Author

Katherine Waite-Gracie is a single, homeschooling mom of two great kids, two fur babies, and a fish called Mr. Malory. Growing up in a small town in Ontario, loving community and nature, she spent most of her time in the water or taking long walks with friends, daydreaming of a life full of wooded, secluded comforts and spending her days and nights with a partner as loving and as passionate about life as herself. Before writing romance novels, Katherine attained degrees and certificates in Intervention, Reiki, and Animal Specialist Programs.

LinkedIn: www.linkedin.com/in/kat-waite-gracie-3681928a
Facebook: www.facebook.com/kat.waitegracie
Instagram: https://www.instagram.com/katsmyth/